Montana Keep

Overloaded with gold, the saddlebags were almost too heavy for their horses and a compelling temptation for greedy eyes. Now Montana Keep and his Shoshone wife, Rain Crow, were caught in a carefully laid trap. Two men followed them. Three others were concealed in timber ahead of them, and another two lay hidden in rocks on either side of the wide gully they were forced to traverse.

Accompanying Montana and Rain was an untested greenhorn and even Montana's fabled skills seemed insufficient to ensure their survival.

In no time at all the Wyoming Mountains were echoing with the explosion of action and the death that would follow.

Montana Keep

Billy Hall

A Black Horse Western

ROBERT HALE · LONDON

ISBN 978-0-7090-8263-7

Robert Hale Limited
Clerkenwell House
Clerkenwell Green
London EC1R 0HT

Typeset by
Derek Doyle & Associates, Shaw Heath
Printed and bound in Great Britain by
Antony Rowe Limited, Wiltshire

CHAPTER 1

It was a long shot, even for him.

Mentally he breathed a word of thanks for the Sharps .50 caliber rifle. It was really too cumbersome to carry on his saddle comfortably. On the other hand, he had relied on it too many times to be without it. He squinted along the top of the barrel. He pulled the rifle back and adjusted the rear sight one more notch. He looked along the sights again. Barely perceptibly, he nodded.

He breathed another sigh of thanks, this time for his friend's bright red hair. That made it so much easier, even from this range.

The high, clear air carried the sounds well. Too well. He could hear every scream issuing from Ian's mouth. The only time the screams stopped, was to fill his lungs with air again, so he could scream some more.

At first, the screams were coherent. They were directed streams of vitriolic expletives. They offered descriptions of his captors, their mothers, their ancestors, the fate in hell that awaited them, everything he could think of.

After while, though, it was just screams. Mindless screams of indescribable agony.

He lay naked in the Wyoming sun. He neither noticed nor cared. He was stretched out on the ground, spreadeagled. Ankles and wrists were bound by rawhide thongs to stakes driven into the hard ground.

Beneath him was a huge anthill.

Red ants.

Huge red ants, whose every bite seared like a hot iron. They swarmed across him in countless numbers. Each bit off a tiny piece of flesh to carry back to the nest. Each injected, as it bit, the toxic substance that burned like fire, eclipsing the pain of the incision of numberless bits of his body.

He writhed and twisted within the constrictions of the rawhide bands. They tore into the flesh of ankles and wrists, but he scarcely noticed. Every movement of his body crushed ants beneath him. The death signal sent out by every dying insect redoubled the fury of the attacking hordes of the tormenting creatures. His screams echoed from the rimrocks.

Only when he had to stop to refill his lungs could the low-voiced, guttural conversations of those watching with evident delight be heard.

Sweat poured from Montana's face. He whipped

6

out a bandanna to swipe it away, then returned to the sights of his rifle.

This was not the way the day was supposed to go. They had left the troop of cavalry before the sun first offered the glow of its promised rising. Colonel Barker knew a sizeable band of Crow were somewhere in the area, bent on raiding ranches and settlements. The unit had been playing cat and mouse with them for almost four weeks. The soldiers' mounts were getting footsore and weary. So were the soldiers.

'Take two days if you have ta,' Barker ordered Montana and Ian. 'Make a wide enough circle you'll cut sign if they've been around. If ya don't find 'em, we gotta head back ta Fetterman.'

They had ridden until nearly evening with no sign of any passing Indians. Then they cut the trail they'd been looking for.

'Only four of 'em,' Ian observed, pushing the US Cavalry hat on to the back of his head.

Montana nodded, studying the tracks. He scratched the stomach of his buckskins absently as he frowned at the ground. 'Scoutin' party, must be. This late in the day, they'll most likely be headin' back to where the others is camped.'

'Should we hightail it back an' let Barker know?'

Montana's frown deepened. 'Mite early. All we know is they's Injuns. Jist four. Don't know what bunch, er if'n thet's all they is.'

Ian looked off in the direction the tracks led. 'I

ain't keen on followin'em. Not now. Ain't enough light left. We'd most likely stumble right inta their camp, long about dark.'

Montana nodded. 'Let's find ourselves a spot fer a dry camp. We'll git some shuteye, an' head out a-follerin' 'em at first light.'

Neither had to mention there would be no fire, no hot coffee, no fresh food. Not tonight. Not in the morning. They were seasoned veterans of the Indian wars.

Ian bore a bitter hatred of the Indians. He had seen enough atrocities to last a lifetime, his first three months with the army. Nothing had happened since to change his opinion.

Montana, on the other hand, felt a profound sympathy for the Indians that tempered his own equally strong loathing. He understood the fear and anger of the land's natives. They had watched the incessant encroachment of their land. They had witnessed the often senseless slaughter of the game on which they subsisted. That slaughter threatened the existence of even the great buffalo that had always seemed as eternal as the mountains themselves. Their entire way of life was being pushed out of the way by a seeming endless tide of white skinned settlers. They knew only one answer. That answer was part of their way of life. They fought. They used every weapon they had. They fought with total disregard for human life, including their own. They fought to instill enough fear, they hoped, to force back the ever encroaching white tide.

Montana had talked of their feelings many long hours with his Shoshone wife. He understood.

On the other hand, these weren't Shoshone. He could tell that much, at least, just from their tracks, the formation in which they rode, the way they refused to allow their horses to pick an easier course when presented with options. Sioux, he guessed. Crow, maybe. Nez Perce, possibly, but not likely. Might be Absaroka.

At first light they began to follow the trail of the four. They rode easily, confident they wouldn't near the quartet before noon at the earliest.

That was the first of their mistakes. It never entered either of their minds that the tracks might be the bait – that they might be the hunted, instead of the hunters. They were midway through a shallow valley when a slight motion along the ridge to their right caught both their attentions instantly.

No hesitation delayed either man. Each shouted a simultaneous warning. Each whipped his mount around and drove spurs into the animal's sides. Each horse leaped forward. Driven by the adrenalin of the fear they intuited from their riders, the horses were running flat out in four strides.

Both men leaned forward, hugging their horses' necks, reducing the wind drag as much as possible, as well as presenting the smallest possible target.

The ground became a blur beneath the rhythmic drumming of their horses' hoofs.

Behind them war whoops erupted. The four Indians who had left the trail were accompanied by a dozen of their fellows. They swept down into the shallow valley in full pursuit.

Montana and Ian had good horses. The best. They refused to ride anything less. It was exactly for moments like this they had chosen them. Slowly, almost imperceptibly at first, the distance between them and their pursuers began to lengthen.

Glancing over his shoulder, Montana smiled tightly. They had caught sight of an over-eager warrior just in time. They had just enough distance. They were out of range. Barely out of range, but winning the race. They would live to scout another day.

Then Ian's horse went down.

It might have been a prairie dog hole. Badger hole maybe. Maybe just a rock the racing animal didn't notice. It didn't matter.

What mattered was that Ian pitched forward, over the animal's head. The horse squealed in pain that almost certainly meant a broken leg.

Montana hauled on the reins and turned his horse around. Ian had already jerked his rifle from the saddle scabbard. He knelt on one knee taking aim. 'Keep ridin'!' he yelled. 'They's too many of 'em!'

Racing back to his friend, Montana yelled back, 'Get up here! Brownie kin carry double.'

Ian's rifle barked. An Indian went down. The others didn't hesitate. Firing as they rode, they began to chew up the ground around the pair with bullets.

'Get outa here!' Ian yelled. 'They'll git us both if'n ya don't go. Now git!'

Montana hesitated an instant longer. Physical pain wrenched from his gut up into his throat. He knew full well Ian was right. If he stayed to fight beside his friend, they would both die. If they tried to ride double, they would be quickly overtaken. Already in range, the bullets from the Indian's guns were working closer.

Ian dived behind a big rock for what protection it offered and yelled again, 'Go! Git movin'!'

Feeling as if his gut would burst, Montana wheeled his horse and clamped the spurs to his sides again. The broken ground and scrubby brush changed to a greenish blur again as the mighty steed regained the rhythm of his stride.

Behind him, Montana heard the furious firing of a dozen rifles, then silence.

He stole a look over his shoulder. Three of the warriors had continued pursuit of him. As he looked, they acknowledged they had no hope of catching him. They wheeled their mounts and returned to their fellows.

Dropping over the crest of a hill, Montana hauled his mount to a halt. Springing from the saddle, he wrenched his rifle from its boot and scrambled back to the crest, careful to keep his presence masked by a clump of sage.

Ian was standing up. His hands were in the air. He was surrounded by nearly a dozen Indians.

Glancing back toward the valley they had fled, Montana picked out four brown bodies lying on the ground.

'Got four of 'em,' he muttered. 'Why d'ya give up, ya moron! Them's Crow. Ya shoulda made 'em kill ya. Or done it yerself.'

Helplessly, he watched as Ian's hands were jerked behind him and tightly bound. He was thrown on to the horse of one of the dead Indians. One of his captors grabbed the lead rope.

As he did, Ian's captor looked toward the hill from which Montana watched. Montana tried to push himself deeper into the ground. He felt the eyes of every brave on him, certain they could see through the brush and grass, even though he knew they couldn't.

After interminable seconds, the leader of the band said something and kicked his horse into motion. They rode off at a gallop, leading the animal upon which Ian sat helplessly.

Montana waited an hour before he began to follow. Even then, he rode more than a hundred yards to the side of their trail, just in case they left a couple behind to kill or capture him if he tried to follow.

They were content, it seemed, to have one captive to make sport of.

They did an admirable job of doing so. They tormented and taunted Ian in a dozen ways. They taught him new levels of pain, before they led him to his ultimate fate. Montana had crept close enough to see the expression on his battered face when he saw the ant hill. He knew what was coming.

Instinctively, Ian's eyes lifted and scanned the horizon around the village. Montana knew he was looking for him, hoping his friend hadn't deserted him to his fate. He also knew better than to try to signal his presence. Ian would see it, but he wasn't the only one.

Montana crept back to where he had tied his horse. He brought him as close as he dared. Then he crawled back to the spot he had chosen.

It was maximum range, even for him. Few men could hope to shoot even the Sharps accurately from that range. He dared move no closer. He would need every yard of distance he could buy. If he failed, or stumbled, or his horse stumbled, his fate would be the same as Ian's.

He looked along the sights of the rifle. 'Hold still, Ian,' he whispered.

As if in answer, Ian stopped his writhing and twisting, for an instant. It was enough.

A Sharps roars like a cannon. It echoes off the rims and rocks of the mountains. It reverberates

13

up the canyons and valleys. It causes all who hear it to stop in their tracks.

In that instant, Ian's body bucked convulsively once, then lay still. The sounds of his screams assaulted the air no more.

Before the sound even reached the village, Montana was moving. At a dead run he returned to his horse and vaulted into the saddle. He probably didn't need the spurs he used anyway. He did need every ounce of speed of which his mount was capable.

Brownie had already been in one life-or-death race today. Although Montana had been careful to water him well and give him as much grazing time as possible, he knew his stamina wouldn't be nearly its normal level.

He hadn't run a quarter of a mile before he heard the first whoops of pursuit. Grimly he marveled at the ability of the Indians to reach their horses and mount a pursuit that swiftly. He only hoped the horses closest at hand were the same ones they had used earlier. That, at least, would level the playing field.

He wasn't that lucky. By the time he had covered half a mile, he could see they were beginning to gain on him. He began to watch for a place to make a stand. He needed a place where he could account for as many of them as possible, and still have time to put a bullet in his own head before they could reach him. Whatever else happened, he swore he

14

would not suffer the things his friend had borne.

The half mile he had run stretched out to three quarters of a mile. He looked back over his shoulder. He was holding his own! They had gained very little, or maybe none, on him. His heart began to race.

He leaned farther on to his horse's neck. 'You're doin' it, Brownie! You're doin' it! Keep it up, boy! Ya kin do it!'

As if in answer, the big gelding's stride seemed to lengthen slightly. His head began to move in rhythm with his hoofs, as if he was deliberately using his whole body to wring out every last bit of speed he owned.

More than a mile now. Montana looked over his shoulder again. Clearly his pursuers were falling behind. They could see it as well. Only the three in the lead continued the pursuit. The rest slowed their horses to a trot, or turned back in disgust.

A mile and a half. Montana glanced back as he topped a low rise. The last three pursuers were just pulling up, acknowledging defeat.

Just in case, he kept the mighty gelding running for another quarter mile before he let him begin to slow. Then he slowed him to a swift trot. He kept up that pace for three more miles. Only then did he dare to find a place to stop, to hide, to let the animal rest enough to continue.

It would be tomorrow before he could report to Barker. That would have to be soon enough. It was enough for one day, just to stay alive.

CHAPTER 2

'Where's MacGreagor?'

Montana ignored the colonel's salute. He despised the military regulations and traditions. Besides, he was a civilian scout. He didn't need to mess with that nonsense.

'Dead.'

Fire flashed briefly in the grizzled officer's eyes. His voice broke the sudden silence like brittle ice shattering on a cold morning. 'What happened?'

Montana took a deep breath. 'We got suckered inta a trap.'

Colonel Barker's eyes continued to bore into him as he waited in silence. Montana began to explain. 'We came on to tracks o' four Indians. Couldn't tell what tribe er nothin'. Waited fer mornin', so's we wouldn't stumble inta some sorta trap. We did anyhow. We spotted one of 'em afore they was ready. We took off a-runnin', an' we was gainin' good. Had 'em outrun. Then Ian's horse went down. I couldn't save 'im.'

'They captured him?'

Montana nodded.

'Can we mount a rescue?'

Montana shook his head. 'Not now. They wa'n't no chance. I kilt 'im.'

The silence of the cavalry troop became suddenly deafening. 'You killed him?'

Again Montana nodded.

Barker glared a hole through him, waiting for the explanation that was not forthcoming. His voice dripped with exasperation. 'When you get around to it, maybe you'd like to explain that.'

When the colonel offered nothing to ease the story, Montana hurried through it. 'I snuck back an' watched from the rim. They worked 'im over plumb bad. Then they stripped 'im an' staked 'im out in a ant hill.'

The collective intake of breath by more than two dozen soldiers sounded like a sudden gust of wind. Montana looked around at all the wide eyes, reading the carefully controlled terror in every one.

'I got where I could, an' put a bullet in 'is brain with my Sharps. Then I hightailed it. Managed ta outrun 'em.'

He could see the conflict work its way through the eyes of the career military officer. To kill a fellow soldier deliberately was a court martial

17

offense, regardless of the reason. At the same time, he well knew the unbearable torture that bullet had saved Ian. He knew as well the immense risk Montana had taken to spare his friend further agony.

He glanced around at the faces of his company. His eyes returned to Montana. 'How long will it take you to lead us to them?'

Montana replied slowly. 'One hard day's ride, maybe. If'n they was where I left 'em, which they won't be. It'll be a matter o' trackin' 'em again. An' sooner er later, once they know we're on their trail, they'll have another trap all set fer us.'

'What makes you say that?'

Montana shrugged. 'It worked once. Then they got cheated outa watchin' an' listenin' while Ian died real slow. They'll be plumb hoppin' mad 'bout that. Wantin' revenge. They'll be wantin' ta do the same to several of us now.'

Colonel Barker pondered the information a long moment. 'We'll ride out at first light. We'll double the number of scouts riding ahead and on our flanks. We will find them, however long we must pursue. We will find them! When we do, we shall exact a just vengeance for their savagery.'

He wheeled and walked away. The others of the troop stood in awkward silence for several minutes. A new recruit finally spoke up. 'Couldn't you have come for the rest of us, so we could've saved MacGreagor?'

18

Montana tried to keep the scorn from his eyes. He reminded himself this was a new recruit. He was from back east. He was used to a different world. He said, as evenly as he could keep his voice, 'It was already too late fer thet.'

The young man frowned. 'What d'ya mean?'

'I mean it was already too late ta save 'im.'

'You mean he'd have died anyway?'

'Oh, prob'ly not, by the time they got 'im ta the ant hill. But he still couldn'ta been saved. By the time they staked 'im out there, it was already too late fer him.'

'That don't make no sense. Why would it be too late?'

'Cuz they'd a'ready done made 'im hurt too much. They know how ta make a man hurt in ways he didn't never even know he could hurt. They kin make 'im hurt in ways he can't never forget. Even if he gets rescued by somebody, he can't never fergit the hurt. He can't never be brave again, cuz he's found out how much he kin be made ta hurt. When a man's been made ta hurt thet bad once, so he screams an' cries an' calls out fer 'is momma, an' promises anything he kin think of, jist ta get 'em ta stop, he ain't never the same. When a man finds out how much he kin be hurt, he knows, deep down, he'd sell 'em his own woman in a heartbeat, jist ta get 'em ta stop, even fer five minutes.'

'I don't think it's possible to hurt that much.'

19

'I hope ya never find out no dif'rent. I seen 'em. I know.'

'He could've still been rescued.'

Montana fought to keep his anger at bay. 'Part of 'im mighta been, if the whole bunch of us was already there. Which we wasn't. Which we couldn'ta been, afore the ants killed 'im. But the best part of 'im was already gone afore they staked 'im out. The only thing, or at least the best thing, anyone could do fer 'im then was put a stop ta the hurt. He'da never been even half a man after what they'd done to 'im.'

'So you wouldn't have rescued him if you could have?'

Montana pursed his lips thoughtfully. 'I don't rightly know. Didn't have ta make thet choice. They wasn't no way ta even come close ta gettin' 'im outa there. Only thing I could have any chance o' doin' was puttin' a end to his mis'ry. So I done thet.'

The private acted as if he would argue further, but Montana cut him off.

'Where's McElroy?' he asked.

After a moment's hesitation, the recruit indicated a cluster of soldiers several yards away. Montana headed directly toward the group. McElroy always had a bottle stashed away somewhere. He seldom indulged, but he'd pay almost anything for a bottle of whiskey tonight.

More than anything else just now he needed

something to rinse his mind of his friend's screams. Those screams still echoed there, threatening to drive him mad.

CHAPTER 3

'They pulled out yestiday a'ready, sir.'

Colonel Barker eyed the young corporal, then looked around. He could not suppress the heavy sigh that rose from his breast. 'Then let's check it out.'

The corporal signaled the troop, and the cavalry surged over the crest of the hill, entering the hollow at a brisk trot. Scattered debris marked the hastily abandoned Indian camp. He held up a hand, halting the company.

Montana had already broken off from the rest. He sat his horse staring at the remains of his friend.

Ian MacGreagor's body still lay spread-eagled in the searing sun. It still swarmed with great red ants, feverishly ripping away bits and pieces of flesh. Already bone showed in several places. The eyes were completely gone. Most of the lips were gone, exposing teeth in a macabre and mirthless grin. Montana shuddered in spite of his best efforts.

'Get a burial detail over here!' Colonel Barker bellowed.

Montana looked at the officer. Ineffable sadness made bottomless pools of his eyes. 'Beggin' yer pardon, Colonel. They'd best wait till after dark.'

'What?'

Montana nodded toward the huge hill, swarming with the angry insects. 'Them's purty fierce ants, sir. If'n anyone tries ta untie 'im, an' drag 'im off'n there, the ants'll be all over 'em, bitin' 'em up so bad they won't be no good at all fer two er three days. It ain't gonna make no difference ta Ian if'n we wait'll dark. Come sundown, the ants'll all go back in their hole. Then we kin bury 'im proper without a bunch o' the boys gettin' all bit up.'

The colonel glared at the scout for a long moment. Finally, unable to argue with the logic, he whirled his horse and fled the gruesome scene.

'Any sign of dead Indians?' he demanded of the corporal.

'No, sir. They must've hauled 'em away with 'em.'

'Have the scouts recon their trail as far as possible and still be back by dark. We'll bivouac on the opposite side of the spring. Have the men ready to move out at first light.'

'Yes sir. Uh, sir. Did you notice the shot Montana made, sir?'

'What are you saying, Corporal?'

'We, uh, I, that is we couldn't help noticin', sir. That's a fifty caliber hole in the top o' Ian's skull. The ridge Montana had t've made the shot from is pertneart five hunert yards over yonder. Got 'im dead center in the top of 'is head. Never felt a thing. Thet's some shootin', sir.'

Rather than answer, the colonel wheeled his horse and rode away, face inscrutable. His men saw no more of him that day.

First light saw the company mounted, waiting the command to move. The scouts, Montana included, had left fully two hours ahead of dawn.

At the colonel's command, Corporal Ferguson ordered the troop forward. They rode out at a brisk walk, passing the mound of fresh earth marking the resting place of Ian's remains. Everybody looked carefully away as they rode past.

The third day they found the fleeing Indians. The band of Crow were confident now that they had eluded any pursuit. They had pitched camp along a stream in a wide, shallow valley. Montana and a young recruit from Tennessee lay in the brush at the brow of a hill, studying the scene.

'Ain't even got no lookouts,' the young recruit whispered.

'Don't need 'em,' Montana whispered back. 'Dogs'll spot anyone afore a lookout would. If'n they thought we was hot on their tail, they'd have a brave up here, an' on all the other high points around, though. They think we gave up. Thet's why they bin joined up by the rest of 'em. Must be pertneart thirty-five of 'em in camp now.'

'They don't know Barker,' the private muttered.

'He's some like a bulldog when he latches on to a bone all right,' Montana agreed. 'Let's ease back outa here an' let 'im know.'

Two hours later they studied a map, hastily drawn in the dirt. 'Couldn't be better,' Colonel Barker gloated.

'I cain't figger how come they're holed up like thet thar,' Will Steiger, the young Tennessee recruit, drawled. 'They's sittin' thar like ducks on a pond, jist a-waitin' fer us to pounce.'

Montana frowned. 'Thet's what worries me. 'Tain't like 'em, gettin' thet careless thet quick.'

'Likely cuz them other two didn't see us,' Will suggested.

'Other two?' the colonel queried, staring at Montana.

Montana nodded. 'They posted a couple o' braves on their back trail, watchin' fer pursuit. We figgered where they might be, an' stayed outa sight. Come up where we could see 'em, without them a-seein' us. Watched 'em two er three hours, till they up an' rode off, follerin' t'others.'

'Ah!' was all the colonel responded.

He studied the map in silence several minutes, then summoned Corporal Ferguson, Matt Wilhelm, and Ford Mattern. Ford was a grizzled veteran whose uniform showed where sergeant's stripes had been removed.

'We'll divide the command into four groups,' Barker ordered. 'Corporal, you take your group and leave at once. Circle wide, and get into position here, where this ridge will conceal your movements.'

Corporal Ferguson nodded his assent. 'Yes, sir. How will we know when to attack, sir?'

'My unit will fire the first shots. When the shooting starts, sweep over the hill. Stay far enough this way that you'll be firing past the unit coming down from the other side. I don't want anyone shooting into our own units.'

'Yes, sir.'

'Wilhelm, you take your group and circle wide the other direction. I want your unit spread out across the creek here, blocking the lower end of the valley. Your unit will stay down, and under cover for the duration, until and unless there are any who attempt to flee past you. If you get too close, you may fall to friendly fire, so keep your heads down.'

'Got it,' Matt replied.

'What?' the colonel demanded.

'Got it,' Matt replied.

The colonel glared daggers through the young soldier for fully half a minute, before his displeasure registered. Matt stammered, 'I mean, Yes, sir. Understood, sir.'

'That's better,' Barker growled.

He turned to the grizzled veteran. 'Sergeant, I want your unit coming straight down the creek, fanned out, ten paces apart. You should encounter their horses. They should be tethered for the night. Try to move past them quietly enough that they are not disturbed, so you will be between the Indians and their horses.'

'I ain't a sergeant no more,' Mattern grumbled. Belatedly, he added, 'Sir.'

The colonel responded, 'You will be tomorrow, if this matter results in the desired outcome. I will personally see your rank is restored.'

Mattern's eyes flashed briefly. 'Thank you, sir,' he said, his voice much crisper.

Barker continued. 'Montana, you will stay with my unit. We will remain in position here, below the brow of the hill, completely concealed from the savages, until first light. As soon as it's light enough to see clearly, we will surge across this hill and descend on them before they have time to prepare any kind of defense. You other units, except for yours, Wilhelm, will move forward with all haste as soon as you hear our first shots. Are there any questions?'

There were none.

'Then, Corporal, you will move out at once with your unit, as will you, Private Wilhelm. Sergeant, your unit will wait two hours, then begin your circuit to bring your unit into position. My unit will

27

move out in four hours.'

The company was quickly divided up into the four units, and two of them rode out at once, moving with surprising silence in the late afternoon haze.

Nobody would ever know why it worked so perfectly. Nobody would understand how a seasoned band of Indians would allow themselves to become so careless so quickly after knowing they were being pursued.

Everybody would remember the morning of that battle. They would try to forget. They would pray fervently that they might forget. They would remember in spite of all their best efforts.

At first light, Colonel Barker waved an arm silently. His unit rode over the brow of the hill, riding toward the hastily erected village along the creek. Even then, they were nearly half way to the scattered tepees before any alarm was raised.

One brave, stepping from his tepee, looked up and saw their approach. He yelled a warning and dived back inside for a weapon.

Well within rifle range, Barker ordered his unit to dismount and commence firing. As Indians began to erupt from their shelters, a withering blanket of fire met them. Most of them never got off a shot.

Instantly, mounted cavalry thundered toward the village from the opposite direction, and downward along the creek. Unlike Barker's unit, they remained mounted, firing as their horses raced toward the ill-prepared defenders.

It was as complete a slaughter as could have been devised. The two mounted units hit the camp at the same time, galloping through it, roping the tops of tepees and ripping them away from those huddled within. As soon as their cover was gone, a hail of lead snuffed the life from the occupants of every tent in turn.

Only two shots fired from downstream. No more survivors than that made it beyond the boundaries of the killing field.

Sudden silence descended. Corporal Ferguson looked around with a wide grin. His eyes roved across the camp until they encountered the form of a naked infant, covered with blood. His grin faded. He turned and threw up abruptly.

Others began to echo his mixture of emotions, as they realized that more than half of the slaughtered Indians were women and children. The young scout from Tennessee fell to his knees, muttering incoherently as tears streamed down his face. He rocked forward and back, hands gripping the sides of his head.

Montana turned wordlessly and mounted his horse. He rode directly in front of Colonel Barker. 'Colonel, I didn't hire out to slaughter women an' kids. I'm givin' my time.'

'What are you talking about,' Barker yelled, much more loudly than necessary. 'These are the savages that tortured your friend. We have gained a stunning victory this day! You should be jubilant!'

Several answers surged to the front of Montana's mind. None found their way through his clenched teeth. He guided his horse around the fuming officer and kicked the animal into a gallop, away from the scene of carnage.

CHAPTER 4

If it appeared anywhere except at the end of a long winter, spring would be intolerable. Dark clouds scudded across the sky, blocking out the sun, sending a chill across the land. The sun would shine just long enough to thaw the frigid edges from long-frozen hopes, before another black cloud hid the land again.

The wind blew. Always, the wind blew. It howled down the mountain valleys. It moaned in the lofty pines. It drove the fading chill of winter through the bones of all whom its icy breath could touch. Brief rains came, driven before the gusty winds. The droplets stung like needles against any exposed skin. They chilled man and animal to the bone.

Rivulets of snow melt skittered across rocks and still-frozen lichen, seeking lower elevations. They joined together, trickle by trickle, until they became rills, then creeks that turned flat valley bottoms into quagmires. They wound their devious ways to larger streams, that turned quickly to raging torrents, swollen with the promise of new life and warmer days. They roared and danced, burying rocks they had detoured around days before. The vibrancy of their song echoed up the slopes of every mountain valley. It bounced from boulder to boulder, pulsed through the thawing earth, beating the ageless rhythm of changing seasons.

Dormant roots of aspen and cottonwood came to life. Stems of buck brush and berry vines began to swell. Sap began moving sluggishly upward to waken myriad dry and brittle stalks and twigs from winter's sleep.

At the edge of a clearing a doe, heavy with new life within her, sought a secluded dale. Finding what she searched for, she lay down to extrude a spotted fawn on to the chilly earth. Rising, she turned at once to begin licking it clean. As she did, she constantly nudged it, hastening to make it stand. Some primordial urge impelled her to force the awkward infant up. She understood, without knowing a reason for her sense of urgency, that it must fill its belly for warmth and strength. It must learn to use its new legs before predators were drawn by the magnet of an easy and succulent meal. It must hurry. It was the birthling's time to do or die. Spring is more deadly than the bite of winter to the young and helpless.

Montana Keep studied the burgeoning signs of

spring and nodded with satisfaction. It had been a good winter. More than a third of his traps had been full every day. He and Rain Crow had worked hard all winter skinning and scraping. They had tanned some, using the brains of the animals. They had stacked most in the shelter he had constructed for the purpose. They had so many the two of them wouldn't be able to transport them in one trip. It would take at least two, maybe three trips down the mountain to the river, where they could load them in canoes for the trip to the traders.

They had worked a good bit harder than he wanted to. Winter was supposed to be a time of tending the trap lines, caring for the furs, but mostly of idle time. Time Rain Crow could use to make new clothes and moccasins for them both. Time to spend enjoying each other, exploring each other's bodies in ever new and creative ways, keeping one another warm through the long, cold nights. Time to talk softly together in front of the fire's glow.

There, alone with him, away from her people and any intruders, was the only time she would open up and share her heart with him. She told him, shyly at first, then with growing boldness, of the strange dreams she had always had of becoming part of the white man's world. Since she had seen her first white women, with their colorful dresses and starched bonnets, she had longed to be like them. She had ached for their freedom to speak in their men's presence. She had marveled at their ability to carry and use weapons, the same as their men. She had envied the evident relationship they shared with their husbands. She coveted the fixed stability of their homes – homes with solid walls of wood and roofs and doors that could be shut against the winter's blast.

Somewhere in the throes of one or another of those long winters he had promised her that chance. Some day. When they had a good enough year. When there were enough furs.

He had thought at first it was just a lonely woman's whim. But the dream stayed, grew, took on its own life. More and more she had begun to press for some timetable, some promise that it might become more than an empty dream.

He had resisted that at first. But the last two or three winters he had begun to change. The ache in his bones grew deeper with the cold of each winter. The catch in his back bothered more often, after handling too many heavy furs. The chill of winter grew more oppressive, spring slower in arriving, summer too short. He began to think maybe Rain Crow was right. Maybe it was time to think about leaving his beloved mountains.

Deep within himself, he knew this was the year. They would never have this many furs again. If the prices were good, they would be wealthy. She was young, much younger than he. She would adapt quickly. They could find a patch of ground and settle down like his own people. He could build a small cabin at first, then expand it each year until it became a house that would satisfy every dream she had. Maybe, then, her body would finally respond and produce that child they both longed for.

His reverie was interrupted by a tiny glimpse of movement down the valley. He instantly disappeared into the timber, as if his presence there moments before had been only an illusion.

Nearly an hour later a lone rider labored upward toward the head of the valley. His shoulders sagged. He looked about himself seldom, trusting his horse to pick the easiest route.

The horse, too, looked weary, as if ridden too many days without time to eat and rest. They passed through a copse of quaking aspens, with buds barely beginning to swell with the urge to put forth leaves. As they stepped into the open a soft voice stopped them in their tracks.

'Long way up the mountain,' Montana's voice drawled.

The rider jerked erect. His head swivelled wildly from side to side. His eyes jumped and darted, failing to find any source of the voice.

Failing that, he spoke. 'Who's there?'

' 'Pends on who yer lookin' fer, maybe,' the voice answered.

'I'm, uh, I'm looking for someone.'

'Wal, ya done went an' succeeded. Ya found

someone. Was ya thinkin' 'bout some pa'tic'lar someone, er jist anyone?'

The rider turned slowly toward the direction the voice seemed to emanate from. 'I'm looking for a mountain man.'

He jumped when the response came from a different direction. 'Now I bet thet thar's the reason you're a-lookin' up here in the mountains. Jist makes sense, it does.'

'A particular mountain man,' the rider corrected.

'Wal, I 'spect I'm 'bout as p'tic'lar as a mountain man kin get. P'tic'lar 'bout how's come a feller come bustin' old snow drifts to ride clear up here, anyhow.'

Obviously discomfited because the voice kept moving, but the rider could catch no glimpse of movement. He could hear no hint of sound, except the voice. He made a visible attempt to stop swinging around, back and forth, trying to keep up with its direction. 'I was told I might find a mountain man called Montana Keep in this region.'

'An' what would ya be wantin' with him?'

'I want to hire him.'

'He ain't likely fer hire.'

'Are you him?'

'Ain't decided yet. Who're you?'

'My name is David Cunningham.'

'Thet don't tell me much. Ya with the army?'

'No.'

36

'Law man?'

'No.'

'Who ya with, then?'

'Nobody. I'm here on my own.'

'An' what business ya got with this Montana Keep that'd fetch ya clear up here this early in the spring?'

'It ain't that early.'

'Must be near April.'

'It's halfway through May.'

'That so? Late spring.'

'I'd have been here a couple months sooner if I could have. Too much snow. I just about killed my horse getting here as it is.'

'I noticed he was lookin' a mite peaked. You ain't sizin' up much better.'

'I have to find Montana Keep.'

'What ya want with 'im?'

'Are you him?'

'Depends on what ya want with 'im.'

Cunningham took a deep breath. 'Like I said, my name's David Cunningham. Last fall, not long before the first big snowfall, a band of Crow Indians attacked a group of wagons. They killed all the men, and a good share of the women. They took some as prisoners. One of the prisoners is my sister.'

A long silence ensued, before the answer came from the trees, in a softer tone. 'Sorry. Thet's gotta be a tough 'un to swaller.'

Cunningham nodded. 'The army tracked them. They were able to get some of the prisoners back. Another attempt was made, through a trader, and the rest were ransomed, except for my sister. They weren't able to buy her.'

'How come?'

'One of the Indians has taken a particular fancy to her. He decided to keep her for his own woman. He won't let her go.'

'Thet happens.'

'I can't let it happen. I can't just leave her there.'

'So your wantin' ta hire this here Montana Keep?'

'Yes.'

'Ta do what?'

'To find her! I have to rescue her from those savages.'

'They might jist kill 'er, 'stead o' lettin' ya have 'er.'

'I know that. I would prefer that to leaving her there with them. I know Laura would too. She would much rather be killed than subjected to the slavery of being some savage's woman.'

After another long silence, the voice said, 'Wal, I 'spect we'd best be gettin' ya ta my camp. My woman's a Shoshone. Thet thar bother ya any?'

'No,' David said at once. 'Not if she's yours by choice.'

Montana chuckled, stepping into the open. David and his horse both jumped when the mountain man appeared as if by magic right in front of them. 'If'n ya knowed Rain Crow even a mite, ya'd know she don't do nothin' 'cept by choice. Let's go get ya some vittles an' git your horse staked out where 'e kin git some grub too.'

He strode off without a backward look. Horse and rider followed, struggling to keep up.

CHAPTER 5

'Ain't no way we kin do it no sooner.'

David looked in turns as if he would cry, then as if he would fly into an uncontrollable rage. His face alternated between reddening as if he were about to explode, and ashen pallor as the color drained from it, leaving his lips colorless. When he spoke, his words were flat and hard, devoid of expression. 'I've waited all winter.'

Montana nodded. 'I know thet. Me'n Rain Crow worked all winter, too. We worked like dogs all winter, fact o' the matter is. We was lookin' forward ta havin' time ta use up all our energies on other things whilst the snow was a-flyin', but trappin' was so good we didn't hardly ever have no energy fer nothin' but work. Tendin' traps. Fightin' snow drifts ten, twelve feet deep. Tendin' furs. Tendin' fires. Tendin' ever'thin' under the sun 'ceptin' each other. Well, we ain't walkin' away from thet thar whole winter's work ta let it sit an' rot.'

'I can make it worth your while.'

'No, ya cain't. Ya ain't got nothin' that'd make it OK fer us ta walk away from thet thar whole winter's work.'

'Money isn't an object.'

'Ain't no object ta us, neither. The land done give us all them furs. They's a dead animal what wore ever' one of 'em. We ain't wastin' all them lives.'

'Nothing I can say will persuade you otherwise?'

'Nope.'

David's colorless lips were a thin, straight line across his lower face. His eyes bored into Montana's. He may as well have been staring down a brick wall. Abruptly his entire demeanor changed. He took a deep breath. 'Well then, what can I do to hasten that process?'

Montana grinned broadly. 'Wal, now, thet ya kin do a right smart deal about. Another hand'll make handlin' all them furs a whole heap easier. We got a passel of 'em.'

'How quickly may we expect to transport and deliver them?'

Montana shook his head, grinning at David's precise grammar. 'Two, three weeks, I reckon.'

David's eyes clouded. 'That long?'

'Thet quick,' Montana corrected. 'Month might be more like it. We got ta git it done whilst they's still two er three foot o' snow ever'where, ta run the sleds on. Ain't no way ta pack 'em outa these

41

mountains after thet.'

David fought the dozen or so questions the statement stirred in his mind. Not willing to appear totally ignorant, he decided to leave them unasked for the time being. Finally he nodded in a visible surrender to the inevitable. 'Well, then, let's get started.'

They got started the next morning. It was the soonest he could prod the imperturbable mountain man into action. They chopped trees and built three large sledges with broad runners and flat decks. A long rope was attached in a loop to each end of all three sledges. At the center of each Montana fashioned a crude harness that would fit around the shoulders and across the chest, allowing the one pulling that sledge to do so with his entire body, rather than with just arm strength.

'Why do you put a harness on the rear end of the sled too?' David asked finally.

The customary grin flashed across Montana's face. 'They's places ya'll figger it out quick enough,' he said. Then he explained anyway. 'She's pertneart all downhill twixt here'n the river. Right steep downhill, some places. It'll take all we got holdin' back agin a sled to keep it from goin' wild an' smashin' agin the rocks er timber. Lot's o' places it'll take all three of us haulin' one sled up a hill, er holdin' back fer all we're worth on one, takin' one at a time.'

'Oh,' was all David could think of to offer.

It took a full week to build the sledges, load the furs, pack up all their gear and distribute it among the sledges. David's impatience was tempered by fatigue. He couldn't ever remember working harder, or longer days. He ached and hurt in muscles he hadn't known existed. Only the fatigue itself allowed him to sleep through the pain every tiny move shot through his body. But by the end of the week, he was feeling better. The soreness was working off. Long unused muscles pulsed with new vitality.

He also learned a swift and profound respect for Rain Crow. He had immediately assessed her round but petite size as making her a hindrance to the accomplishment of their goals. The first day they worked together he watched, sometimes open-mouthed with amazement, as she lifted things far heavier than he could manage. She moved bales of furs immovable by him. She chopped down a tree while he was making a notch in the side of one. She had its limbs removed before his own tree landed in the snow. At the end of the day, he could barely move with exhaustion. His hands trembled with the weakness of fatigue. She had done far more work that day than he. Nevertheless she went about preparing and serving them supper, moving with the same grace and agility with which she had begun the day.

To avoid the chagrin of being so badly outworked by a woman, he employed a mental gymnastic of assuming Montana had somehow found himself a super-human anomaly for a wife and partner. Then he corrected himself sternly. Squaw. Not wife. She's one of those savages. They don't marry, like civilized people. She's just his squaw.

By the end of the week he looked at her in a whole new light. She never spoke in his presence, but at night, before the exhaustion swept him away into the blessed oblivion of sleep, he could hear them conversing, sometimes in English, sometimes in Shoshone. He realized she was Montana's equal in ways he would never have imagined. He was surprised at the way that fact stirred anger within him that he did not understand. He didn't have much time to think about it, though. The demands of every day and the fatigue of every night left little time for musing.

Just over a week after he arrived, they left the crude but cozy hut in which Montana and Rain Crow had spent the winter. Their horses were laden heavily with packs. Each of them had a sledge to tow. David bit his tongue rather than ask the reason for that arrangement. It seemed to him that it would be more sensible to use the horses to pull the sledges, then they could pack all the stuff on them and walk freely.

He was glad he had suppressed his urge to suggest that when they began the first long slope down the mountain.

Just before they topped the rise that fell away in a steep, nearly mile long incline, Montana halted. He was towing the lead sled. Rain Crow followed, with a sled loaded every bit as heavily. David came last, with a sled loaded more lightly. The lead rope that led to the three horses was attached to the rear of his sled.

Montana summoned both of them, instructing David to grab the rope on the rear of his sled, as Rain Crow had already done unbidden. When they had a firm grip, he pulled the sled forward. As it rocked over the lip of the rise, it began to slide on its own. Instantly Montana jumped to one side, flipped his rope on to the top of the stacks of furs, then grabbed the restraining rope with the other two. Together, the three dug in their heels, hauling back with all their might, to impede the forward surge of the sledge.

The hill was steep and long. Within seconds they were leaned back against the rope, being propelled forward down the slope at a terrifying speed. Their feet dug into the snow, making furrows with wakes of snow rolling to the sides, as they fought their losing battle to slow the sled's descent.

Two thirds of the way down the slope, David's foot struck a rock hidden beneath the snow. It stopped his foot instantly. The rest of his body was not so fortunate. He flipped forward into the snow. Losing his grip on the rope, he somersaulted, rolled, bounced and slid for more than a hundred yards. Regaining his feet, he lumbered through the snow after the fleeing sled, racing faster now that it was only impeded by two people. He caught up with them only after they reached the bottom of the hill.

They all stood, gasping for air, for several minutes. Montana finally asked, 'Ya OK?'

'I think so,' David puffed, still gasping for air.

'Didn't bust your ankle er nothin'?'

'I don't think so. No. I'm sure I didn't. It hurts a little. Not much.'

'Lucky. Thet kin snap an ankle slicker'n snot.'

'I didn't even see what I hit. Must've been a rock under the snow.'

'Most likely. Ain't no way ta see it, neither. Jist be ready ta roll if'n it happens. If'n ya roll quick enough, it won't bust nothin'. 'Less ya hit somethin' a-rollin', thet is.'

David changed the subject. 'Is that why you don't use the horses to pull the sleds? Because they can't get out of the way when it starts downhill?'

'Yep. Sled'll run over 'em. Bust their legs. Goin' downhill with horses, ya got ta have a reg'lar harness, an' staves, an' a brake o' some sort. They'll have a hard enough time gettin' down these big hills with jist the packs. They go uphill a whole lot better'n down, with a load.'

At Montana's word, they struggled back up the hill. At the top they huffed and puffed until they had all gotten their breathing back to normal, then repeated the process with the second sled. When the third sled was at the bottom, they each brought a horse, careful to stay to one side so they did not, themselves, get run over. Even with the snow still deep on the slope, the horses struggled to remain under control down the mountainside.

When the entire assemblage was at the bottom, they resumed their previous stations, lugging the reluctant sleds forward.

Two hours later they were faced with an uphill battle. 'She ain't as steep uphill as she looks,' Montana encouraged. 'Ever'thin' else bein' downhill makes it look more uphill than it really is. It's some uphill though. Time to do some real work.'

David bit his tongue, choking back the retort that challenged what they'd been doing all day. By the time the three, pulling together on each sled, had finally pulled and hauled all three sleds to the top of that rise, he understood the accuracy of the mountain man's assessment.

In the bottom of the next valley a spring fed a small stream that quickly grew with snow melt. They camped there for the night.

David marveled again at the incredible stamina of the Shoshone woman. So tired from the day's work he could scarcely stand, he watched her go about setting up their camp, building a fire, cooking their supper as if she had done nothing else all day. By the time Montana had taken care of the horses, she had supper ready. They ate swiftly and silently. In minutes after they finished, they were all three wrapped in their bedrolls, sleeping in anticipation of another grueling day to come.

CHAPTER 6

Without looking at Montana, she spoke softly, in Shoshone.

Just as softly, with no visible response, Montana replied in English. 'I seen 'em.'

David looked from one to the other, frowning in confusion. Taking his cue from them, he spoke just as softly. 'Is something happening?'

Montana leaned against the furs stacked and secured on the sledge. Appearing to anyone observing to be merely catching his breath, he spoke with his head down. 'Couple fellers taggin' along behind us.'

David resisted the urge to jerk his head around to look for himself. With great effort he copied Montana's attitude, leaning forward with his hands on his knees, seeming more out of breath than he actually was. 'Why?'

'Steal our furs,' Montana replied curtly. 'Whole heap easier'n trappin'. They'll likely wait'll we get 'em near ta the river, then take 'em.'

From the questions that tumbled over each other in his mind, David selected what seemed the most pertinent to ask. 'How many?'

Montana directed his response to his wife instead of answering. 'You make it two, Rain Crow?'

As she busied herself tightening the ropes securing the furs she said, 'Three. Two watch us. One stays out of sight. Not always same two that watch.'

Montana snorted softly through his nose. 'Bein' plumb sneaky, huh? Keepin' one back outa sight, jist in case we spot 'em. Then if'n I try ta s'prise 'em, they'll s'prise me instead. Gotta be thet 'breed.'

'He is one,' Rain Crow confirmed.

'Who is "the 'breed"?'

'Half-breed mangy coyote calls hisself Joe Dog. Half Nez Perce by a French trapper. Nasty customer.'

'So what should we do?'

'Let's pitch camp.'

'It is early,' Rain Crow protested.

'Yup, but not too early. They'll figger we're jist too tired ta make a full day out've it. I want enough daylight ta take keer o' things afore it gets plumb dark.'

'How are you going to do that?' David demanded.

'I'll handle thet end o' things,' Montana assured

him. 'You jist help Rain Crow git camp set up. Keep your ears an' eyes peeled. Listen ta Rain Crow. She'll tell ya if'n anyone gits close. I'm dependin' on you ta keep 'er safe. I'll jist sorta dis'pear here in a minute er two.'

Standing straight, pretending to stretch his back, David risked a quick glance around at the top of the ridges that surrounded him. When he looked back, Montana had disappeared. Trying to register no surprise, he set about to help the Shoshone woman set up camp.

CHAPTER 7

Spring comes to the south slopes first. The thin, dry air of high altitudes offers little resistance to the sun's direct effects. Even more than ten degrees below freezing, direct sunshine begins early to eat away at the deep blanket of winter's snows. On those open south sides of hills and mountains, the snows melt and wildflowers begin to herald the coming summer while the snow remains several feet deep everywhere else.

In the timber it doesn't make nearly so much difference. The constant shade of tall pines, spruce and firs shields the deeply drifted snow from the sun's powerful rays.

As Montana, Rain Crow, and David Cunningham were wearing snowshoes, the south slopes and bare, exposed stretches were avoided. It would be easy enough to slip off their snowshoes, sling them over their shoulders, and walk where there was little or no snow. It would be a far different matter for the heavy sledges bearing the bundled results of a very fruitful winter's trapping. They needed that snow to make it possible for them to pull the sleds. On bare ground, they would be unable to budge them at all.

Those furtively following the trio had no such need. They were able to cover greater distances with ease. They stayed below the ridge line, where they would never be visible to the straining, laboring transporters of the precious furs. As they needed, they could crawl to the top of a ridge and watch them, keeping close track of their progress, waiting for the right time, the right location, the right situation to strike.

Because they avoided as much of the snow as possible, they also left less trail for anyone to follow. At least, most would have found it so.

Montana Keep, on the other hand, needed no trail that most trackers would have required. The signs of the others' passing was as clear to him as the trail of ink across a white page. Even from a distance, keeping within stands of timber where the snow was deep, where even the sun would never see him, he studied the pattern of their activities.

He saw where and how the third member of the group hid and watched while the other two moved to where they could keep watch of the furs and those who owned them.

He watched the careful surveillance that third

member maintained of the most likely path anyone stalking them would take.

He observed the setting of the trap that had his name on it, as surely as if it were graven on a brass plate.

'Knowed good'n well either Rain Crow er me'd spot 'em,' he muttered to himself. 'Countin' on it. Waitin' fer me to come after 'em so's they kin bushwhack me afore they go after the others. Gotta be Joe Dog, all right. Jist the sorta thing he'd think of.'

He watched the three patiently until the sun slid behind the western peaks, and long shadows slid across the ground.

He waited as the almost instant chill replaced the warmth of the fleeing sun's rays. He felt the thawed surface of grass and snow turn swiftly crisp and frozen, waiting the warmth of tomorrow's sun to renew its inexorable shift toward spring.

He observed the three as they realized their quarry was making camp for the night. Unseen, he fixed carefully in his own mind every detail of the surroundings of the camp site they, in turn, set up for themselves. He made special note of where that third man settled down, wrapped in blankets, to watch. That was the one he wasn't supposed to know about. That was the one who was there just for him, Montana.

They knew him. At least Joe Dog knew him. They had no doubt he would come after them, that he would have spotted them. They were ready.

They were not ready for the keen eyes of Rain Crow. She alone had noted that the two watching them were not always the same two. She shouldn't have been able to tell that. Not at that distance. Not with just those fleeting glimpses they deliberately allowed to alert them that they were being followed. Not with that faintest offering of bait that few other than Montana Keep would ever even notice, let alone respond to.

Jack McReady positioned himself carefully. He was perfectly concealed within the stand of timber. In front of him, the only feasible approach to the campsite where his two fellows were, lay clear and open. Especially in the wash of moonlight, it would be impossible for even a mouse to approach that campsite without his awareness.

He hugged his blankets closer around him against the approaching night's chill. He wished for a passing moment he had put more blankets beneath him. The icy tentacles of the frozen earth were already finding their way through those that were there. He knew better than to move to correct the situation, however. He knew the reputation of Montana Keep. If, as Joe Dog insisted would happen, Montana had spotted them and was stalking them, he would surely hear or see any movement. It was best to endure the cold.

His fingers wiggled on the Colt .45 in his hand beneath the blanket. He needed to keep his fingers loose. If this was the night Montana showed up, he would need to shoot quick. He could do that. He had done that half a dozen times before. His victims had never known he was there. They died with that ignorance intact, never knowing why or from where their deaths had come.

He smiled tightly at the thought. The smile abruptly disappeared. He heard something. The tiniest of noises, too small and swift to identify. It was something, though. He was sure of it.

Careful not to move any part of his body except his eyes, he cast about swiftly, then more slowly and carefully. He looked for anything out of place. He watched for any fleeting shadow. He waited for another sound. His fingers tightened on the Colt.

Suddenly a hand reached around each side of the tree he leaned against. One grabbed his head, jerking it back. The other brought a razor sharp knife across his throat, nearly severing his head from his body.

A fountain of blood blossomed in the moonlight. A soft gurgling sound sputtered from his severed windpipe. His hand squeezed spasmodically on the Colt beneath the blanket. Even muffled in the wrapping of the blanket, the shot echoed and bounced against the silence of the night.

Sound erupted for an instant from the spot his two fellows slept. Montana cursed once, softly. Silence descended again on the mountainside.

After ten minutes of that silence, a voice whispered softly. 'Jack? You get 'im?'

Montana fixed the position of the speaker in his mind, not moving. He was not much concerned about him. That he would speak, especially now, marked him as inexperienced. Not that dangerous a foe.

Not so with Joe Dog. Montana knew exactly how dangerous he was.

Instantly when Jack had fired a dying shot into the ground through his blanket, Montana had back-pedaled swiftly into the trees. He picked a spot with a wide patch of brush behind him. In the moonlight it looked far too thick to be breached silently. It would have to do.

He crouched right in the edges of that brush, watching, listening, waiting.

When the whispered query sought for McReady, he did not move. The passing shadow of an owl that had returned to its summer haunts early flashed briefly and was gone. Somewhere a small animal scraped against a twig, making it rub another in the most insignificant of sounds.

Half an hour crawled past. No other sound broke the silence. Montana did not move.

The wind picked up slightly, rustling branches, sighing softly through the needles of the pines.

To his left, a shadow moved almost imperceptibly. His face and body motionless, Montana shifted his eyes, watching intently. The shadow moved again. He looked the other way, casting swiftly around for the second enemy.

The smallest of sounds carried on the night's silence from some place the other side of where he knew the dead man lay. Sudden relief surged through him. One at a time. They were separated, trying to move against his hidden position from two directions. They had guessed wrong. He wasn't between them.

The silent shadow at his left moved again. As it flitted across a narrow slice of moonlight he recognized the form of Joe Dog. He focused his attention entirely on the movements of the half-breed.

As silently as a passing thought, the hunter moved from tree to tree. After every step he stopped, watching, listening. Montana willed himself invisible, forced himself immovable, demanded himself impossibly patient.

The path of Joe Dog's movement was as close to him as it was going to get. The half-breed faced directly away from him. Montana rose to his full height silently. He stood for half a minute, waiting for blood to rush back into his legs, cramped from crouching more than an hour.

Satisfied his legs would obey him, he moved forward in a silent rush. The large knife that had nearly severed McReady's head was held low in his right hand. His left hand extended before him. He moved as noiselessly as the shadow of the owl had passed, swift as death itself.

Even so, some sound, some instinct, some breath of air reached Joe Dog. He whirled, his own knife arcing outward, just as Montana reached him.

Montana grabbed the wrist with his outstretched hand at the same instant he felt Joe Dog's hand grip the wrist of his own knife hand. He twisted sideways just in time to avoid the uplifted knee aimed at his groin. He aimed a kick of his own at his stalker's knee, and was thrown slightly off balance when it connected only with the air where the knee had been an instant before.

Silent as a dream the two strained against each other's grip, kicked and parried at one another, tried every ruse and trick they knew to throw the other momentarily off guard. For either of them, it would only take an instant. It would require only the slightest error.

As their desperation grew, so also did the sounds their struggle emitted. Montana knew with increasing fear that the third member of the group must have already heard them, must even now be hurrying to help his comrade dispatch him.

Abruptly Joe Dog used both his and Montana's grip on each other's arms to pull Montana toward him. Instead of resisting, Montana twisted slightly and lunged toward his assailant.

The twist once again thwarted the aim of the uplifted knee. As he rammed against the would-be killer, he slammed his head forward, smashing his forehead into Joe Dog's face, catching him right on the bridge of the nose.

Joe grunted, and relaxed for the barest instant. It was enough to allow Montana to drive his own knee upward into his opponent's groin, lifting him clear of the ground for an instant.

Still gripping each other's wrists, he jerked Joe toward him, smashing his head into the other's face a second, then a third time. He felt the grip on his wrist begin to relax.

He drove his knee into the other man's groin a second time, jerking his hand out of the other's grip at the same instant. His hand came free.

A scuffing sound behind him sent alarms stabbing through his mind. Still gripping Joe's wrist, he jumped sideways, jerking Joe around into the spot he had occupied an instant before. Joe stiffened as the knife, intended for Montana's back, penetrated his instead.

He straightened spasmodically, stretching up to full height, his mouth open in a silent scream.

In the instant it took the third of his hunters to realize what had happened, Montana stepped around the rigidly upright form of Joe Dog and drove his own knife upward under the rib cage of the would-be back-stabber. The man gasped loudly, jerked his knife out of the back of Joe Dog and turned to face Montana.

Montana backed away two steps, watching. The man grabbed for the gun at his waist, trying with swiftly failing strength to pull it from its holster. It was more than his dying body could accomplish. He crumpled to the ground at almost the precise moment as Joe Dog. Two lives drained into the frozen soil together.

'Shoulda used the gun to start with,' Montana scolded the dead man. 'Ya'da had me, sure's anythin'.'

He called out to Rain Crow and David as he approached his own camp. After so narrowly escaping death, he didn't want to die now by being mistaken for his enemies.

CHAPTER 8

It took a full week to build a raft to Montana's liking.

It certainly wasn't to David's liking, even then.

'There isn't any way that thing will float this much weight.'

'Aw, I reckon it's big enough.'

'It's big enough all right,' David grumbled. 'Too big. Way too big to control in water that fast.'

'Too big to upset goin' over a rock, too.'

'But big enough to get hung up on rocks so it can't move.'

'Maybe,' Montana agreed reluctantly. 'Not likely, though. Snow melt's runnin' full bore. There oughta be a deep enough, wide enough channel all the way.'

'What if there isn't?'

'Then we'll git hung up some.'

'So let me take the horses and meet you there,' David urged. 'That'll take away more than two thousand pounds of weight, give the raft a shallower draught, and I'll meet you and Rain Crow at the trading post.'

Montana shook his head quickly. 'Take ya too long. We kin be there in a couple o' days, way the river's runnin'. It'd take ya more'n a week with the horses. If'n ya made it at all.'

'I made it up to find you.'

'Ya got close enough I found you,' Montana corrected.

'I would have found you.'

'Maybe. 'Bout a year from next winter. 'Less'n I didn't want ya findin' me.'

David changed tack. 'The horses are not going to submit to riding this contraption down the river.'

'They ain't gonna have no choice, once we git a-goin'. They's gonna be way too busy keepin' their feet to worry 'bout nothin' else.'

'I don't like it,' David insisted.

Montana studied the young man. 'You a-skeert o' the water, boy?'

David felt the blood rush to his head, turning his face bright red. 'It, it isn't just that,' he protested. 'I just don't think it's a good idea to put your whole winter's work on this huge conglomeration of logs lashed together with ropes that will soak up and weaken, even if the horses don't panic and knock us overboard or upset the whole thing.'

'Skeert o' the water,' Montana affirmed. 'I

reckon ya kin jist git over it. O' course, if'n ya don't wanta come along, I'll be thankin' ya fer the help an' sayin' "So long".'

David sputtered. 'But . . . but you have to help me find my sister. That's what this whole thing is about from the beginning. I have to find her! I have to.'

'Then I reckon ya hafta ride this here river.'

Montana turned his back and resumed loading the bundles of furs, lashing them all firmly in place. Three narrow spaces were left in the center of the large raft for the three horses. In that space there were three loops of rope. Each had been run around one of the logs that formed the raft. They provided a ready spot to tether each horse. With the firmly lashed bundles of furs on either side of each horse, they would be prevented from falling, even in rough water.

David cast about in his mind desperately for some argument that would dissuade the mountain man from this nonsensical course of action. It wasn't until he caught Rain Crow watching him with an unaccustomed small smile that he gave up the effort. If he died in the course of this insane adventure, it wouldn't be with some squaw smirking at his cowardice.

At first light the next morning they led the reluctant horses on to the raft. They secured the sturdy halters to the ropes provided. 'Let's shove off,' Montana ordered.

Untying the ropes that held the raft in place, David lunged aboard. It took only seconds, it seemed to him, for the current to catch the craft. It propelled it and him downstream at a terrifying rate.

Standing spraddle-legged, Montana gripped the long pole secured to the rudder. As if he had spent a lifetime doing so, he guided the conveyance to the middle of the rushing, tumbling stream.

David thought he was going to be sick. He fought down the churning of his stomach valiantly. He would rather choke on his own vomit than give that smirking Indian woman anything more to denigrate him about, even in her mind.

The ride was relatively smooth for the first thirty minutes. The horses began by rolling their eyes, ears laid back tightly against their heads. Slowly they began to relax, soothed as much as anything by the constant crooning of Rain Crow. She kept a soothing tone, mouthing words David could not understand. Neither did the horses, but they understood her tone. They understood the firm, calm hands, stroking them as she spoke.

Then they hit the first stretch of rapids. They heard the roar of the turbulent waters before they saw them. By that time it was already too late to do anything but hang on and hope.

The raft bucked and rolled, but stayed upright. Ice-cold spray soaked them. Rain Crow grabbed the rudder pole along with Montana, helping him fight to keep the craft pointed toward the spots that appeared to promise the greatest chance of passage.

Three times the bottom of the raft struck rocks. Each time it hesitated, shuddered, then slid on across, propelled by the fierce currents.

In minutes, that seemed like hours to David, they were past the rough stretch and into relatively calm waters again. Immediately Rain Crow hurried to the horses, working to calm them again. One at a time, beginning with the most frightened, she rubbed them down with gunny sacks and restored their sanity.

By that evening, enough other streams had joined the one they rode to provide deep enough water for smoother passage. By the time they merged into the Platte River, nearly twenty hours from the time they launched, they were all relaxed and confident.

Rain Crow and Montana took turns at the tiller, allowing each other to catch brief snatches of sleep.

Several times during the trip they spotted people on shore. Three times they were groups of white men. The other times they were Indian.

Twice they were fired on, but they were moving too swiftly to worry much. The river, swollen as it was with snow melt and spring rains was more than a mile wide. They were far more worried about sand bars or rocks than bullets from the shore.

As darkness crept across the sky the second day of their trip, they spotted the fires and torches of Deer Creek Trading Post.

At once Montana grabbed the tiller and moved the craft to shallow water, to the lesser currents along the shore, allowing it to slow. He beached it a hundred yards above the trading post.

As it struck ground, David bounded ashore, gripping a pair of ropes. He dallied the first around the base of a tree trunk, then sprinted to another tree to secure the rope from the raft's other end. He had never in his life felt anything as wonderful as firm ground beneath his feet. He silently vowed never to set foot on another river raft as long as he lived.

Only after the craft was secured did he look around. He was surprised to see a crude fort, and a substantial encampment of soldiers immediately behind the trading post.

'The army is here,' he announced.

Montana merely nodded. 'They pertneart always is, this time o' year. Indian agents an' fur traders both want 'em.'

'Why?'

'Too many furs. Too much money.'

'Whose money? I don't understand.'

'We ain't the only trappers in the country. They come here from a fer piece to sell their pelts. Lots of 'em, like us this year anyhow, want it in gold. Indians'll trade furs fer a few guns er ammunition er whatnot. Trappers want gold an' supplies. The fur traders always hire their own little army too, but they want the reg'lar army here if'n they kin git 'em. Keeps 'em alive longer.'

As he spoke, a detachment of four soldiers approached. Montana grinned as he recognized one of the four. 'Ford Mattern, ya dried up ol' galoot,' he greeted the one with sergeant stripes. 'I figgered ya'd either died o' old age er been drummed outa the army by now.'

'Howdy, Montana,' Mattern drawled. 'Looks like a good winter.'

'Best I ever had in my whole life,' Montana agreed. 'Wait'll ya see them pelts. Prime, ever' one of 'em.'

'Big enough raft to float a regiment.'

'She took the ride in good shape, too,' Montana beamed. 'Rode 'er like a river rat.'

'Who's your passenger.'

Montana's grin didn't change, but he noticed the instant scowl that clouded David's face. 'Thought ya'd met my woman, Ford. This here's Rain Crow.'

'I know her. Who's the other fella.'

'Aw, he's some greenhorn done got hisself lost up in the mountains. I offered ta let 'im ride down with us, in exchange fer helpin' us sled the furs down ta the crick.'

'That so?'

Mattern turned to David. 'What's your name?'

he demanded.

David knew instinctively that his quest to find his sister would not meet with military approval. He had just survived the most terrifying experience of his young life. He was tired. He hurt in more places than he thought he owned that could hurt. He was in no mood to be questioned by some non-commissioned officer of obviously inferior birth.

David scowled back at the sergeant. 'David Cunningham. What's yours, Napoleon?'

Mattern's face darkened instantly. 'Don't get smart with me, Junior,' he growled. 'I'll have you in the stockade till you get a civil tongue in your head.'

'On what charge, Sergeant?' David demanded. 'Is it suddenly illegal to fail to bow and scrape to anyone wearing a military uniform nowadays? If I am not mistaken we have fought a couple wars explicitly to rid ourselves of that attitude. But if you wish, I can certainly discuss the matter with your superiors. I'm sure most of them will be well aware of my family's name and connections.'

'I don't give a rat's hind end fer your name or your connections,' Mattern insisted. Nevertheless his expression changed noticeably. Whether that stemmed from David's obvious education or claim to belong to a prominent family wasn't as easily discerned.

'What was you doin' up in the mountains?'

'Minding my own business, Sergeant. Does that

concern the military?'

' 'Pends on what your business is.'

The young man drew himself to full height, fixing the sergeant with a look of withering disdain. 'Exploring the length and breadth of this great land for which our forebears have sacrificed so nobly,' David expounded. 'Surveying whether it is truly a land worthy of greater things than being infested with unwashed hordes of the ignorant, the savage, and the hollowly pompous. Duly authorized to report such assessments back to the representatives of the president himself, I might add. I trust it will not be necessary to include any unpleasant appraisals of any malapropos improprieties or breaches of military decorum and procedures on your own part with that report.'

Clearly uncertain and confused, Mattern turned back to Montana. 'He doin' anything the army oughta know about?'

'Spendin' way too much time goin' to school an' hob-nobbin' with high an' mighty mucky-mucks is all, fur as I know. I reckon thet thar country he was lookin' over woulda kilt 'im, if'n I hadn't stumbled onta 'im, though. Them thar high country blizzards wasn't none impressed with all them thar big words an' high connections.'

Mattern glared at David. 'Neither am I, as a matter of fact. I'll be watchin' you.'

David declined to respond, so Mattern turned back to Montana. 'Me'n the boys here'll keep an eye on your stuff, if'n ya wanta get some shut-eye, or whatever.'

'Much obliged,' Montana responded. 'I reckon we'll do that. We'll jist sack out on the raft, though. Who's the trader?'

'Still Crenshaw.'

Montana nodded. 'His gold's as good as anyone's.'

'Keep your eyes an' ears open once ya git it,' Mattern cautioned. 'Several hardcases hangin' around, watchin'.'

'We'll be keerful,' Montana promised.

The size of his winter's catch was sure to be noticed. Everyone within ten miles would know about it by morning. It made them a valuable target indeed.

CHAPTER 9

'So where'd you get a name like "Montana Keep"?'

Montana glanced sideways at the young man, before resuming the roving of his restless eyes. Those eyes constantly scanned their surroundings, ever restless in their search for who knows what.

'Trapped up in Montana a few years,' he responded.

'I guess I had rather assumed that much,' David responded. 'It was the rest of the name that strikes me as rather odd.'

Montana almost smiled. 'Story behind thet thar,' he acknowledged.

'I guess I had rather assumed that as well. I was hoping to hear the story.'

Without interrupting the restless searching of his ever-moving eyes, Montana said, 'Spring o' fifty-one. I was comin' down outa the high country, skiddin' a purty fair winter's catch down to whar I could float 'em down. Small bunch o' Shoshone s'prised me. Six er seven of 'em fronted me, afore I even knowed they was around. Figgerin' I didn't speak Shoshone, the leader o' the bunch says ta me, "We take furs".

'Wal now, I wasn't about to jist turn over a whole winter's work thataway. I warn't in too good a spot, neither, though. An' truth ta tell, I didn't really think 'bout what I was doin'. I jist got plumb mad. I jist kept on walkin' pertneart like I didn't hear 'im, an' walked right up plumb agin 'im. Thet thar warn't what he was 'spectin', I kin tell ya. Then I real sudden stuck a knife up agin' 'is throat, an' grabbed a real good handful of 'is manhood with my other hand an' started squeezin' an' twistin' some. I said, "Montana keep furs".

'His face got plumb dark, an' 'is eyes was pert-neart bulgin' outa his head. He looked this way an' that, tryin' 'is best ta figger out how ta let the rest of 'em finish me off afore I could slit 'is throat or tear ever'thin' off I was a-twistin' on. He sorta croaks out, "Montana keep".

'Now figgerin' a Shoshone was most likely a man of 'is word, I says, "Good choice," an' let loose of 'im.'

'He stood there a'lookin' at me fer a minit, tryin' hard ta git 'is voice back. Then he nodded 'is head an' said it agin. "Montana keep".

'After thet, we sorta got ta be friends. I ended up goin' off ta their village a while after thet. The feller offered me 'is sister, an' I took 'im up on the offer. She's been my woman ever since.

'They all called me "Montana Keep" for a while, as a sorta joke on Runs Plenty, Rain Crow's brother. After while it jist plumb got ta be my name.'

They rode in silence for a long while, when David said, 'What was your name before you came west and started trapping?'

Montana glanced at the young man briefly. 'How old ya be, son?'

David frowned. 'Almost thirty.'

'If'n ya aim ta make thirty-one, they's some questions ya oughta not be askin' in this here country.'

David opened his mouth to pursue the subject, then wisely thought better of it.

They had ridden several hours when David said softly, 'Have you noticed the two that seem to be following us?'

'We noticed,' Montana confirmed.

'Do you know who they are?'

'Nope. I 'spect I know what they are, though.'

'What they are?'

'Ne'er-do-wells. They're most likely after the gold we got fer the furs.'

'Ah.'

'They ain't likely alone, though.'

'They aren't?'

'Not likely. I got a bit of a reputation, in case ya hadn't noticed. Ain't likely two of 'em'd take on the three of us.'

'So what are they doing?'

'Waitin'.'

'Waiting for what?'

'I 'spect they got three er four others, at least, ridin' hard ta swing around an' git ahead of us. When they find a spot they like, they'll brace us from the front. Likely have at least two fellers hid alongside somewhere. Then we'll have the two behind us. Then they'll make their play.'

'So what do you intend to do about it?'

'Fall fer it.'

'Fall for it?'

'Best way ta smell out a trap is ta step into it.'

'Isn't that also the best way to be caught in a trap?'

'Yep.'

David's frustration made him audibly sputter. 'But . . . well . . . I. . . . You don't intend simply to yield to their demands, do you?'

'Nope. 'Twouldn't do no good nohow. They ain't likely ta leave us alive, even if we gived 'em the gold.'

'So what are we going to do?'

'Wal, ya reckon ya kin take care o' the two behind us, when things start ta poppin'?'

'Well, yes. Of course.'

'Then when ya hear me say, "Now," git off'n thet horse head first, find whatever ya kin fer cover, an' take care o' them two. Me'n Rain Crow'll worry 'bout the rest.'

He would have pursued the matter, but Rain Crow spoke. He didn't understand what she said, but Montana nodded. Without turning his head, Montana spoke to David. 'Ya see thet draw up ahead?'

'Yes.'

'We're headin' ta go right down it. They got a fella lyin' out on both sides, 'bout thirty yards up the side hill. There's at least three hidin' in the trees at the other end. Thet thar's whar they're fixin' ta s'prise us.'

'The ones behind us are getting closer too. They're trying to stay out of sight, but not doing a very good job of it.'

'Likely want us spottin' 'em. If we're watchin' them, we'll be less likely ta spot t'others.'

Thirty yards farther on, Montana said, 'We'll make our play about fifty yards on. Thet thar'll put us a bit this way from where they're wantin' us. You'n me'll dive inta the cover an' start pickin' 'em off. Rain Crow'll take off on a dead run an' circle around. She'll start workin' on 'em from behind.'

David thought of several objections, but managed to voice none of them. He was still considering doing so, when Montana said, 'Now!'

Before the word was completely out of his mouth, Rain Crow reined her horse to one side, kicked the animal in the sides, and, bending low over his neck, yelled louder than David would have believed possible in the horse's ear. The startled horse spun to the right and lunged forward, carrying the Shoshone woman apparently away from the impending fray.

At the same instant, both Montana and David dived from their saddles, rifles gripped firmly in their hands.

To Montana's surprise, David's rifle barked first.

The two who had been so long trailing the trio had spurred their horses forward as the intended prey approached the mouth of the trap. At the bark of David's rifle, one of them threw his hands up with a yell of pain and surprise and flopped backward on to the cantle of his saddle, then off on to the ground.

He had not yet hit the ground when David's rifle barked again, and the second man slumped over the saddle horn. He wheeled his horse and spurred the animal desperately away, but stayed in the saddle only about thirty feet before he slid to the ground, his life ebbing swiftly away into the Wyoming soil.

At almost the same instant as David's second shot, Montana's Sharps .50 roared. One of the attackers who thought himself well hidden in the timber at the far end of the draw was propelled backward from his concealment, dead before he hit the ground.

'Three down,' David said, his voice edged with excitement that hinged on glee.

'Watch fer the feller on the left,' Montana

muttered as he sighted across the Sharps, watching for any hint of motion from the trees.

As if on cue, a puff of smoke rose from a clump of brush on the side hill ahead and thirty yards to the left of their position. As the bullet from that quarter tore through the twigs just above his head, David's rifle responded three times in rapid succession. The second of the three shots was followed by the unmistakable thunk of lead plowing into flesh.

Montana's Sharps roared again, and was answered by a scream of pain and dismay from the cover of the trees.

Almost as if in response, a blood-curdling scream erupted from the hillside ahead and to their right. It ended in a gurgling gush, followed by an eerie silence. Montana chuckled. 'I think thet thar feller jist met my woman.'

'I don't think he liked her,' David grinned, sighting along his rifle at the trees, watching for any movement.

Hoofbeats of a running horse, crashing through brush and branches, marked the abrupt departure of the last of their attackers.

'Do you think that's all of them?' David asked, still watching the trees across his rifle sights.

'Thet matches my count,' Montana said.

'I'll check the one on the left,' David offered. 'I'm sure I hit him, but I don't know how good.'

'Keep your head down a-goin',' the mountain man advised.

David did exactly that. He started by checking the two who had been trailing them, assuring himself they were both thoroughly dead. Then he circled carefully, approaching the hidden man's concealment from the upper side.

Before he got there, he could see the man's boots protruding from the tall grass surrounding a scrub bush. He approached carefully, his rifle at the ready. When he was thirty feet from him, he was able to see that one of his shots had taken off nearly half the man's head where he lay hidden.

Still leery of any remaining assailants, he returned the way he had come. When he got back to his horse, Montana and Rain Crow were standing beside their horses, talking.

Montana watched him approach. 'Are they all accounted for?' David queried.

Montana nodded. 'They was all dead 'cept one in the timber yonder. Had 'is arm tore 'most off. Rain Crow took care of 'im. Ya want a scalp er two fer souvenirs?'

David shook his head much more vigorously than he really needed to, much to the amusement of both the mountain man and his wife.

It was a couple hours later that Montana said, 'Thet thar was a heap easier'n I had it figgered.'

'Why is that?' David wondered aloud.

'Hadn't seen ya in a scrap yet. Didn't rightly figger ya'd be much account. Ya acted like maybe ya'd been in a tight spot er two. Ya done good.'

David didn't answer. He really didn't know what to say. Even less did he understand the glow of pleasure the mountain man's words caused to spread through him. The glow was still there two days later when they left Rain Crow with her people and rode out on the mission for which David had spent the last several anguishing months. Try as he might, he could never quite get the image of his sister being abused by her Indian captors out of his mind.

At least now, he assured himself, the days of her having to endure that were numbered. He vowed that he would end the misery of her captivity. If it cost him his life, he would end that.

CHAPTER 10

His whisper was soft. 'Is her hair red, like yours?'

'Flaming red.' David whispered back.

'Lookit over ta the far side, comin' this way,' Montana breathed softly.

David shifted the focus of his telescope, sweeping back and forth, then stopped abruptly. His whole body tensed. Trembling shuddered through his frame. He was completely unaware of the soft groan that welled up from his throat. Both of them centered her in the circle of the view of their telescopes.

They lay in thick brush, just below the crest of a ridge. Their faces and hands were smeared and daubed with mud and berry juice. From more than three or four feet distance, they were indistinguishable from the brush and leaves around them.

It had taken them a full hour to crawl from the top of the ridge to their current vantage point. Below them, perhaps 300 yards away, a Crow

81

village sprawled along a small creek. In a clearing thirty yards beyond the village, half a dozen children played some kind of game. One old man sat in front of a lodge, wrapped in a trade blanket, watching them play.

In groups of three or four, the women of the village were busily at work. It was impossible at that distance to distinguish what most of them were doing. In one of the groups, a woman with bright red hair worked with two others. It was there that their gaze was focused. They appeared to be scraping a hide that was stretched out on the ground, held in place by more than a dozen small stakes.

As they watched, one of the other women turned toward her, apparently saying something they could not hear at that distance.

In response, the redhead rose instantly, picked up what appeared to be part of an animal's entrails, and walked toward the creek. Her clothes were tattered and torn. She was barefoot. Nevertheless, she held her head high and walked straight and tall. She knelt at the edge of the creek and held the object down into the water.

'What's she got?' David whispered.

'Deer bladder, looks like,' Montana breathed back, then shook his head slightly. 'Nope. Too big. Gotta be a buffalo bladder.'

'What for?'

'Water.'

'What?'

'Water jug. They use 'em ta carry water, till they commence ta rottin'.'

'For what?'

'Anythin'. Drinkin', most likely.'

'They drink out of an animal's bladder?'

Watching through the telescope, Montana muttered, 'Works plumb fine. Helps some if'n ya rinse it out a mite first.'

David nearly choked on his response, and directed his attention back to the girl, so he didn't see Montana grin as he looked at him from the corner of his eye.

The girl rose from the creek bank, holding the now-filled bladder and walked quickly back to the other women. She handed it to one of them. The other took it and tipped it up, pouring a stream of water into her mouth. She passed it to the other one, who also drank, then dropped it on the ground.

The girl grabbed it and held it up, pouring a small stream of water into her own mouth. The woman nearest to her cuffed her smartly on the side of the head, causing her to drop the bladder. The rest of its contents drained out on to the ground.

She did not respond to the blow, except to drop to her knees and return to scraping the hide.

David spluttered for several seconds, trying to form words. 'Did you see that?' he whispered hoarsely, as soon as he could control his anger enough to form the words.

'Hsst!' Montana reprimanded him. 'Keep it quiet! If'n one o' them dogs hears us, we're dead meat.'

'They wouldn't even let her drink!'

'She let 'er have a couple swallers afore she cuffed 'er.'

'Why didn't she get a drink at the creek if she was thirsty? She was right there.'

'They'da seen 'er.'

'So what?'

'So one of 'em woulda likely beat 'er some, takin' a drink afore she brought them some.'

'Why?'

Montana shrugged. 'Cuz they kin. They kin abuse 'er in small ways thataway, an' git away with it, so they do. I don't 'spect they like 'er none.'

'Why not? What's she done to them?'

'Caught their man's eye, most likely.'

'What?'

'Them two's likely one man's wives. She's with 'em, helpin' 'em do their work. Thet means he's likely laid claim ta her too.'

'Why would you think that?'

'She's still alive.'

'What's that supposed to mean.'

'Thet means one o' the braves staked out a claim ta her. Took 'er as one o' his wives. If he hadn't, she'd belong to every man in the village, ta use as they see fit. She wouldn'ta likely survived this long, if'n thet was the case. They's right hard on a white woman, if she don't git claimed by someone right away. 'Specially a right, smart lookin' one like your sister. They'da used her plumb ta death in a couple er three weeks.'

'That's barbaric!' David protested.

Montana shrugged. 'It's their way. Ya kin be plumb thankful one of 'em staked a claim to 'er.'

David's response was closer to a growl than anything. 'Thankful some savage is abusing her at will?'

'Better'n a couple dozen seein' who kin do 'er the most or the roughest. He's likely plumb fond of 'er, judgin' by the way t'others ain't abusin' 'er none.'

'Whatd'ya mean?'

'Well, they let 'er drink afore the one cuffed 'er. She didn't cuff fer hard enough ta leave a mark. Thet must mean if'n they treat 'er bad enough fer their man ta notice, he'll beat 'em right smart. Thet means he's fond enough o' your sister thet 'e don't care if'n he makes t'other two mad or not. Prob'ly treats her a mite better'n he does them, matter o' fact.'

'How far do you make it?'

'From here?'

'Yeah.'

'Three hunert fifty yards. Maybe closer ta four hunert.'

After several minutes of silence, 'Can we get closer?'

'I been lookin'. Thet thar draw what opens up thirty, forty yards behind an' ta the right of 'em . . . see it?'

'Yeah.'

'Might be we kin slip up there an' be a good chunk closer. Have to check the wind right careful, though. That'd be close enough one o' them dogs'd catch wind of us if we ain't real awful careful.'

'Let's try it.'

Slowly, as soundlessly as possible, they wormed their way back into the brush, then turned and crawled over the crest of the hill. Once out of sight of the village, they looked around carefully for several minutes, then rose and trotted down into the bottom of the draw.

Their horses stood where they had left them, tied to trees in the thickest part of the dense growth that fed on the extra moisture that clung to the bottom ground.

'We best take 'em with us,' Montana declared.

David nodded silently. As he untied his horse and prepared to lead him down the draw, he suddenly turned to Montana. 'Where were all the men? The only one I saw was that one old guy.'

'Huntin', likely. Thet or off on a raid o' some Shoshone er Brule village.'

'No way to know when they'll be back, I don't suppose?'

'Nope.'

'So we have to get our business done quickly and get out of here.'

'Fast'n far,' Montana agreed.

They hid their horses as close as they dared, then began their approach from the new direction. The crawl at the end of that approach was slow and tedious. Some insect bit David behind the ear. He dared not react or swat at it. He carefully, quietly followed the mountain man, who moved like a silent shadow over the lip of the draw, toward a clump of young blackberry bushes.

It was now nearly an hour since they had left the vantage point from which they had spotted David's sister. They peered cautiously through the tall grass at the three women again. Less than fifty yards from them, the three, all with their backs turned, were busily scraping the inside of an elk hide. They appeared nearly finished with the job.

Montana glanced sideways at David. His eyes opened wide, startled. David was sighting down the barrel of his Winchester, finger on the trigger.

Reaction was instantaneous and decisive. With lightning speed, Montana grabbed the rifle, shoving his finger beneath the hammer to prevent its drop on to the firing pin. With the other arm, he rammed an elbow sharply into David's jaw, knocking him unconscious.

Cursing beneath his breath, Montana watched the women. They appeared to have heard nothing.

He squirmed backward, lowering the hammer

87

on David's Winchester. He grabbed the young man's foot, dragging him back into the shallow draw, out of sight of the village.

Clear of the village's vision, he raised to a crouch, dragging the unconscious man as rapidly as possible into a thick clump of brush. He watched their back trail as he gasped for breath.

When he had sufficiently recovered, he knelt and slapped David's face three times.

Mumbling incoherently, David stirred, then blinked, then opened his eyes. Then he tried to sit up with a start, wide eyed.

Montana shoved him roughly back to the ground. His hand on David's chest kept him pinned there.

'What in the Sam Hill ya tryin' to do?' he demanded.

David, though still somewhat groggy, was belligerent. 'What I came to do,' he gritted.

'Ya cain't kill a whole village all by yourself, even if'n they ain't many men around.'

'I wasn't trying to. Just her.'

'Her who?'

'Laura.'

'Your sister?'

'Of course.'

'Now why'n thunder would ya go an' do thet?'

'What else would you have me do? Rescue her? Take her back home? For what? What kind of life could she ever have now? We both know she's ruined. She's been with those savages for months. No decent white man will ever touch her. No civilized society will ever accept her. No church will even allow her in the doors. She's ruined. Ruined. The best thing I can do for her is to put her out of her misery. I can at least take her beyond their ability to continue to use and torture her.'

Montana glared at the young man. Several times he opened his mouth to speak, then closed it again. Finally he said, 'Ya best git on thet thar horse o' yours an' vamoose. I ain't sure why I'm even lettin' ya do thet. But I'll tell ya this: if'n I see thet thar pompous rear end of a' jackass you're wearin' fer a face agin, I'll blow it plumb off'n your head. Ya hear me?'

David rubbed his aching jaw tenderly. His forehead wrinkled in concentration, pulling down into a 'V' between his eyes. 'I don't understand.'

Montana's eyes bored holes through the young man. His words were soft, intense, edged with a steel that made David shudder. 'I don't 'spect ya do. Don't 'spect ya'd understand if'n I tried ta tell ya. You're jist plumb ever'thin' thet right an' decent folks hate about white people. Even worse, ya cain't begin ta figger out how come ever'one in the world don't think jist like you do. An' it ain't my job ta try ta fix thet sick mind o' yours, so I ain't gonna try. Jist light outa here an' don't ya never let me see your face agin.'

David's face reddened as Montana's words

ripped into him. His jaw clenched. His eyes flashed. He whirled and strode to his horse. Mounting, he spun the animal and rode away up the draw.

Montana continued to glare at him until he was clear out of sight. When he was gone, Montana stroked his chin thoughtfully, then set out at a trot to where he had already noticed the horses remaining at the camp were being held.

CHAPTER 11

One young boy was all there was. He guarded the horses casually. They had no need to wander. The grass was knee high. The water was clear and cold in the creek. The main body of horses were gone with all the men of the village, wherever they had gone. The dozen or so remaining were completely relaxed.

The boy guarding the horses was hammering on a piece of flint, studiously working on the forming of an arrowhead. He never looked up. He heard nothing.

Montana walked up silently behind him. He cuffed him sharply across the side of his head. The boy fell to the ground, unconscious. 'Sorry 'bout the headache your gonna have, young'un,' Montana murmured.

Just as silently he worked his way to the best looking of the horses, grazing near the edge of the brush and timber. Like the boy guarding him, the horse never realized anyone or anything was near until the loop of Montana's lariat settled over his head.

As it did, his head jerked up. He snorted. He lunged away, until he felt the familiar grip of the noose around his neck. Then he wheeled, facing his captor. His ears were laid back flat against his head. His nostrils flared. He braced his feet, pulling against the rope.

Speaking softly, Montana crooned an endless string of phrases and words in the Absaroka tongue, hoping to soothe the animal with the accustomed sounds.

It worked. The horse quickly settled down, allowed him to approach, then quieted quickly beneath the reassuring touch of his gentle hand.

Montana looked around quickly. The boy still hadn't stirred. The other horses had snapped to attention briefly, but had already returned to cropping the lush grass, ignoring them.

Moving quickly, Montana led the horse back to his own. Using a piece of his lariat, he fashioned a crude hackamore for the animal. He tethered it to a tree, then slipped out of sight as soundlessly as a fading dream.

In minutes he was once again on the low rise just behind the three women. Staying out of sight of the rest of the village, he spoke softly, again in the Absaroka language.

'Do not make any sound. We will kill anyone

that makes a noise.'

The three stiffened at the sound of his voice, then craned to look over their shoulders.

Again in Absaroka, Montana said, 'We have come for the white woman. Keep quiet, and we will not have to kill you.'

He waited for just a moment, to be sure they were going to comply. Then he spoke in English. 'You're Laura Cunningham?'

With only a sharp intake of breath, Laura nodded her head.

'Then I want ya ta stand up an' walk over like you're headin' inta the brush ta relieve yourself. Come right back this way.'

As if afraid she might waken from the impossible dream at any moment, Laura stood.

'You other two keep a-workin' on thet thar skin,' Montana ordered in Absaroka.

Instantly the two women resumed scraping an already cleaned and finished hide.

'Hurry it up,' Montana hissed to Laura.

With obvious effort, Laura walked directly toward his voice. As she reached him, Montana motioned her to keep walking over the small rise, into the draw.

One of the two Indian women looked over her shoulder and started to stand. Again in Absaroka, Montana hissed, 'Git back to work on thet hide!'

The woman whirled back to the hide instantly. Even as she did, Montana was already moving silently backward. As soon as he was below the top of the rise, he rose and ran quickly in a crouch.

Without saying anything, he grabbed Laura's arm, propelling her along with him. She started to resist and opened her mouth to speak, then changed her mind and ran with Montana. As soon as she did so, he released her.

Rushing into the copse where the horses were tied, Montana gestured toward the Indian pony with the makeshift hackamore. Without a word, Laura leaped to the horse's back and grabbed the ropes that served as reins.

Already in his own saddle, Montana turned the horse and rode directly away from the village. Laura stayed close behind.

Before they had traveled a hundred yards, he heard one of the woman scream and then begin to jabber at the top of her voice. The other woman chimed in immediately. Bedlam erupted in the village.

Montana kicked his horse into a run, noting by the sound of the other horse's hoofbeats that Laura was keeping pace.

He turned and looked back over his shoulder. The young woman was leaning forward, almost flat on to the horse's neck. Her face wore an expression of mixed anguish and joy. Her feet drummed the sides of the horse with every step, desperate to extract every ounce of speed from the animal that it was capable of giving.

They ran the horses flat out for more than a mile. Then Montana steered his horse toward a stream that babbled busily over its rocky bed. Maintaining an angle downstream, he entered the water. Guiding his horse to the center of the stream, he rode downstream for nearly a hundred yards.

Abruptly then he turned his horse and headed in the opposite direction. He silently motioned Laura to do the same. She nodded mutely and turned her horse to follow directly behind his.

Riding more slowly and carefully to avoid disturbing any rocks in the stream bed that could be noticed, they rode upstream for well over a mile. A broad expanse of black shale changed the texture of the shoreline dramatically. Beyond it, still moving upstream, the ground was barren and rocky.

Only there did Montana guide his mount ashore. Still guiding their mounts carefully to avoid any sign of their passing that could be detected, they rode away at right angles to the stream.

Three-quarters of a mile later he turned downhill, away from the difficult going of the rocky terrain. Within 300 yards they passed on to hard, dry ground. Buffalo grass cushioned the ground, providing deceptively nourishing grazing for animals. Scrub sage dotted the landscape, broken at irregular intervals with clumps of larger brush, an occasional aspen grove and thickets of scrub cedar.

Kicking the horses to a swift trot, they set about to put as much distance as possible between themselves and the pursuit that was certain to come. Neither had spoken since Laura had walked away from her captors.

Three hours later, Montana's head snapped up. 'Look out!' he yelled.

As he yelled, he swerved his horse abruptly into Laura's, who had slowly advanced until she was riding almost exactly beside him.

Laura gasped. A bullet whined like an angry bee past her head. They both kicked their horses into a run, as the report of a lone rifle slapped against their ears.

They dropped into a ravine, out of sight of the would-be sniper. The instant they dropped below the rim, Montana leaped from the saddle, his Sharps .50 gripped in his fist. He scrambled swiftly back to the edge of the gully.

Glancing this way and that, he crawled sideways to a clump of sage he could use for cover. Then he raised his head enough to study the spot from which the shot had come.

After several minutes, he pushed the Sharps through the brush, aimed carefully and fired. The roar of the big rifle reverberated across the hills, followed by a suppressed yell from the hilltop toward which he had fired.

Watching closely as he chambered another round, Montana was rewarded with the sound of running hoof beats. Following the sound, he was ready when the fleeing horseman appeared for a brief instant, just ahead of a finger of timber that jutted down from a rocky ridge.

The instant they appeared, the Sharps roared again. The horse went down instantly, throwing the rider forward on to the ground. Recovering his feet, he scrambled quickly behind cover.

'Who was that?' Laura asked anxiously at his shoulder. 'Have they found us already?'

Montana looked around at the strikingly beautiful young woman. He spoke to her for the first time since her escape. 'Nope. 'Twasn't them. They'll likely hear the shots, though, if'n they've come back from wherever they was. They'll be on our tail in a hurry if'n thet's the case.'

Ignoring the threat of his words, she pressed the issue. 'Who was it, then? Who tried to kill me. And who are you?'

He studied her for a long moment before answering. He took a deep breath. 'Name's Montana. Montana Keep, they call me.'

'I'm Laura Cunningham.' Then she added lamely, 'Well, I guess you know that.'

He nodded without answering.

She continued to insist on understanding. 'So why did you come after me, and who just tried to kill me? Did you kill him?'

'Thet thar's a lot o' questions,' he evaded.

Her eyes blazed, showing the first fire of an indomitable spirit since her rescue. 'So start answering them,' she demanded.

He looked at her for another long moment before responding. He was moved by the resolute determination in her steady gaze. 'You are some kinda woman,' he admired.

She ignored the compliment. 'Please answer my questions,' she demanded.

He took a deep breath. 'All right, but ya ain't gonna like the answers.'

'Try me.'

He nodded. 'Wal, like I said, my name's Montana. Your brother hired me ta find ya.'

'David did? Where is he? Where's David?'

'Wal, I 'spect thet thar was him.'

'Where? What do you mean, "him"? The one who tried to kill me? That him?'

'That him,' Montana confirmed.

'Why would David try to kill me?'

'I stopped 'im killin' ya at the village. I thought he wanted ta rescue ya. He didn't. He wanted me ta find ya, so's he could kill ya.'

Her eyes searched his, frantic, confused, hurt. 'David tried to kill me? Twice? Why?'

'He figgers ya bin ruint by bein' a Indian's woman. Figgers thet thar's a fate worse'n death, an' no help fer it no more. So he set out ta do what he figgered was puttin' ya outa your misery.'

98

She opened her mouth several times to reply, then closed it silently each time. Tears welled up abruptly, spilling over, coursing down her cheeks. They left dirty channels marking their path. 'He ... he thought I'd be better dead than Two Feather's wife?' she breathed.

'Yup. I reckon.'

'He thought I'd be better dead than rescued, though?'

'He didn't think anybody'd ever be able ta fergit ya was with the Indians a while. He figgers ever'one hates 'em as bad as he does.'

'But, but he's ... he's wrong! Isn't he?'

' 'Course he's wrong,' Montana growled. 'Now we gotta git movin'.'

'What about David? Did you ... is he...?'

'He ain't dead,' Montana answered the question she couldn't ask. 'I done shot 'is horse out from under 'im. He's got a right smart walk ahead, if'n he's man enough ta make it, an' kin keep hid from the Absark thet's lookin' fer you.'

She probed his eyes with her own for several heartbeats. He said again, 'We gotta git.'

She looked away and nodded. Skirting well away from the timber where David almost certainly waited for another opportunity to shoot his sister, they rode quickly and steadily.

Well after dark, still riding at that ground-eating trot, Montana spoke again. 'I 'spect we kin ride a bit easier now.'

'We can? Why?'

'We're well inta Shoshone country now. Two Feathers ain't likely to chase ya this fur.'

'Is Shoshone country better?'

He chuckled. 'It's a whole heap better if'n ya ain't a Crow er a Sioux er Absarak. My wife's a Shoshone.'

'You're married to an Indian woman?'

'Yup. Fine woman she is, too.'

'What's her name?'

'Rain Crow.'

'What happens then?'

'What?'

'Where are we going? What are you going to do now? With me, I mean.'

'Headin' fer my wife's village, first off,' he explained. 'Thet's whar I left her. We kin hole up there fer a spell. You'll be safe there. Then we'll figger out where ya want me to take ya.'

Even as he said it, he knew that was a whole lot more complicated than it should have been. Thanks to David. If he survived. If the rest of Laura's family felt the same as he did. 'If a whole heap o' things,' he complained silently.

CHAPTER 11

Laura's eyes cast about wildly as they entered the village. Nobody greeted or called to them. An eerie silence enveloped the apparent haphazard arrangement of tepees. Faces peered from those tepees, but well back from the entrance flaps, almost invisible in the dim interior.

'Are, are you sure this is all right?' Laura whispered urgently.

Montana's face showed no response. Just as quietly, he said, 'It's fine. They either ain't sure who ya is, er what's goin' on yet, er they're fixin' ta welcome ya.'

'Isn't your . . . your . . . wife here?'

'She's here. We done passed her tepee. She said howdy.'

'She did? I didn't hear anything.'

'Oh, she didn't say nothin'. Jist nodded ta me, from back in the tepee.'

'And you could see that?'

101

'I was watchin'.'

'Oh.'

Near to the center of the village he reined in his horse. Watching him, confusion and fear etched on her face, Laura followed suit. They sat in silence for nearly five minutes.

Abruptly a Shoshone warrior stepped from a tepee. He was resplendent in buckskin leggings fringed with feather streamers down the outside of both legs. He wore a breastplate made of the hollow leg bones of porcupines. His torso was greased with some kind of fat, making his skin shine. He wore a war bonnet containing more than fifty eagle feathers. Its band was decorated with brightly colored bird feathers, porcupine quills, beadwork and horse hair. He carried a tomahawk in one hand, and a large bow in the other. A quiver of arrows was slung over his shoulder.

His moccasins were soft buckskin, with high tops. They were covered with laboriously sewn beadwork in intricate designs.

The design in the moccasins exactly matched the beadwork that covered the breechcloth that hung from his waist.

He spoke to Montana in Shoshone, speaking slowly with a clear, deep voice.

Montana turned to Laura. 'He welcomes you to the village. He is Night Wolf, head warrior of this village.'

'He is the chief?' Laura asked.

Montana shook his head. 'Shoshone people only have one chief. Each village has a head warrior. Night Wolf is the head warrior of this village.'

Laura, visibly fighting for composure, responded in hopes the Absaroka mores of courtesy were close enough to the Shoshone's to keep her from making a major gaff. 'Tell him I am grateful for his courtesy and hospitality, and for preparing for my arrival as if I were a person of importance, instead of just a worthless woman that has been rescued from captivity by a brave friend of the Shoshone.'

Montana nodded, surprise and appreciation visible on his face. He repeated her message, translating accurately, because he well knew that Night Wolf understood English as perfectly as he, and suspecting Laura understood much of what Night Wolf said as well. The differences between the Shoshone language and that of the Absaroka were not that pronounced.

Night Wolf listened in polite silence, then responded in Shoshone. Again Montana interpreted. 'He says you are too modest. A woman so beautiful, personally chosen by Two Feathers for his wife of love, is a great woman of strong medicine. To have such a one taken from a feared Absaroka warrior and brought to a village of the Shoshone is a great coup for the Shoshone. You are welcome among us as long as you wish to remain. If you choose to leave our village, six of my finest warriors will escort you safely to whatever place you choose to go.'

A gasp of relief and delight escaped Laura's lips before she regained her composure. With a deep breath, struggling to keep her voice steady, she said, 'I am deeply honored to be given so great a welcome, of which I am unworthy. I cannot imagine that I would ever choose to leave a village as great as that of Night Wolf. If I should ever choose to do so, it would only be to spare you the danger of war with the Absaroka of Two Feathers who search for me.'

When Montana had interpreted her response, Night Wolf said, 'The Absaroka are not so foolish as to seek you here, among the Shoshone. If they do, their scalps will decorate our tepees, and you will be given the privilege of taking the scalp of Two Feathers with your own hand.'

Laura's chin lifted at the thought, even before Montana translated the words, giving evidence she did, indeed, understand everything Night Wolf was saying. The fact was not lost on Night Wolf as well, but he continued to address her only through Montana. To have had such a conversation directly with a woman in public would have been too great a breach of customs to even consider.

When the formalities were over, Laura was invited to share the tepee of Montana and Rain

Crow, and promised that if she chose to stay among the Shoshone she would have her own tepee, an honor his tribe had seldom, if ever, conferred upon a woman.

Night Wolf wheeled and disappeared into his tepee. Montana and Laura dismounted. Immediately two young boys appeared from nowhere to grab their horses' reins. Unasked, they led the horses to Montana's tepee. They unloaded Montana's horse, handing his things to Rain Crow. That done, they took the horses to be kept with the rest of the villagers' mounts.

Once inside the tepee, Rain Crow fed Laura a large meal, then showed her the bed already prepared for her. Laura was asleep almost before she had settled into the softness of the thick hides.

Montana was grateful she was exhausted enough they need not worry about waking her. He and Rain Crow had a lot of catching up to do.

CHAPTER 12

Montana's eyes flew open. He wasn't sure what woke him. He didn't question his instincts.

Swiftly and silently he dressed, grabbed his rifle, and slid out through the flap of the tepee. Neither Rain Crow nor Laura stirred.

Outside the tepee, he looked quickly around. Three others, besides Night Wolf, had responded to whatever had wakened him, and stood outside their own tepees, weapons in hand. Night Wolf motioned three different directions with circular sweeps of his arm. With each motion a warrior moved that way and quickly vanished into the pre-dawn darkness. Montana moved silently over beside the village's head warrior. Neither spoke, listening carefully, eyes and ears probing into the lingering night.

A faint noise, borne on the morning breeze, stiffened both men. It was an almost inaudible clink of a bridle bit, carried in the stillness from some distance away.

Instantly Night Wolf began to move through the village, stopping to speak softly into the flap of each tepee. By the time he returned to where Montana waited, warriors were materializing out of the darkness, scantily dressed but well armed.

With a series of hand motions, Night Wolf informed them of the direction of the approaching danger, and deployed those he wished to various positions. Then he and Montana moved directly toward the soft noise that had alerted them.

Behind them, women and children slid furtively from their tepees and disappeared into the brush and timber surrounding the village. If some enemy force attempted to surprise them in their sleep, they would launch a surprise attack on an empty village.

Three hundred yards from the village, a group of mounted soldiers moved slowly forward. A grizzled sergeant nudged his horse forward a little faster, until he was beside the leader.

'Lieutenant, we'd best be makin' some noise,' he said softly.

The young lieutenant glanced scornfully at the older man. 'Why is that, Sergeant?'

'We gotta be gettin' close to the Shoshone village.'

'I would presume so.'

'So we'd best be makin' a little noise,' the

veteran insisted.

The lieutenant sighed indulgently. 'And exactly why would their proximity require us to make noise?'

'On account o' if'n we don't, they's gonna think we're sneakin' up on 'em. If'n they think we're sneakin' up on 'em, we's likely to wake up dead all of a sudden, 'cause the only ones what sneaks up on 'em is enemies.'

'And exactly how is it that they are going to even know we're here, until we announce our presence, Sergeant?'

'Oh, they'll know, Lieutenant. They'll know. Even if'n Montana wasn't there, they'd know. Ya jist don't go sneakin' up on a whole village o' them Indians. 'Specially Shoshones. I s'pect they know we're here a'ready.'

'Sergeant, you've been reading too many dime novels. Indians are not super-human, nor blessed with super-human senses. They will be totally and utterly surprised at our presence, when I choose to announce it. I give you my word.'

Suddenly, as if materializing from the ground itself, a half-circle of Indians stood up from the tall grass. Horses squealed in fright. Soldiers cursed. One young private screamed in terror, grabbing for his sidearm.

Into the sudden bedlam, the quiet voice of Montana drawled, 'Ya oughter listen to an old soldier once in a while, ya stupid shavetail.'

The young lieutenant probably didn't hear his words. He was far too busy trying to keep his seat. His mount squealed in terror when Montana stood up from the grass less than two feet in front of him. He reared high into the air, his eyes rolling, his ears laid back flat against his head. When his front feet returned to the ground he tried to wheel and flee, held in check by the reins that pulled his chin nearly back to his chest. Terrified and frustrated he began bucking and plunging, first this way, then that. The lieutenant abruptly lost the battle to stay in the saddle. He cartwheeled in the air, landing flat on his back. The force of striking the earth drove the air from his lungs, leaving him helplessly flailing, struggling to breathe.

Before the terrified horse had fled more than a dozen steps, a strong brown hand grabbed the flying reins and wheeled the animal around. The Shoshone warrior gripped the side of the bridle, holding the horse in an iron grip, and began speaking softly to him in Shoshone. The firm grip and calm voice penetrated the animal's panic, and he began to settle down, a little bit at a time, as he pranced a circle around the immovable Indian.

Meanwhile the rest of the soldiers had realized instantly they were surrounded by armed warriors, and had lifted their hands in visible assurance that they had no evil intentions. Sergeant Ford Mattern sat his already steadied mount, a broad grin spread clear across his face. 'Howdy, Montana,' he said.

Affecting a stern pose, Montana addressed the grizzled veteran. 'Mattern, how's come ya cain't keep this ignorant little pup of a shavetail from tryin' ta git 'is whole outfit kilt thataway?'

Ford shook his head ruefully. 'It ain't fer lack o' tryin', Montana. Some o' these—'

As if on some inner signal, his hand whipped up to his shoulder, fingering the newly replaced sergeant's stripes, and his words cut off in mid-sentence.

After a brief but obvious silence, he continued, 'Some of the unseasoned officers find it hard ta believe things ignorant old fools like me tell 'em. I'm sure he'll turn out to be a fine leader o' men with a little experience.'

Montana laughed aloud at the sergeant's feeble attempt to cover himself. He raised a foot and jabbed the still gasping lieutenant in the ribs, considerably harder than he needed to, to get his attention. 'What're ya tryin' ta do, Lieutenant, git your first command all kilt?'

The lieutenant sat up with an effort, his eyes darting around at the scowling warriors in obvious panic. 'What . . . where . . . how. . . ?'

Montana interrupted his stammering. 'Did ya figger ya could jist ride right in on a Indian village an' they wouldn't never even know ya was there?'

The lieutenant swallowed noisily. 'I, we, I mean, uh, I didn't think we were making enough noise for anyone to hear us.'

On a whim, Montana raised his head and translated the lieutenant's words into Shoshone, loudly announcing them to the circle of warriors.

Following his cue, the Indians laughed uproariously, as if they had just heard the funniest story ever told. They began to repeat the words back and forth to each other, laughing again every time the statement was repeated.

The lieutenant shrank visibly, casting around at the circle of warriors, his mouth sagging open in shame and amazement, his face as red as the dawn sky.

After the razzing had gone on for several minutes, Sergeant Mattem spoke up. 'Montana, we do have some serious business what's brung us here. I s'pect maybe we'd best be tendin' ta that.'

Under his breath he said, 'Afore Lieutenant Wilson loses all hope o' regainin' 'is command. He's got the makin's of a good officer, Montana. 'E really does.'

Glancing across the disconcerted faces of the soldiers, becoming visible now in the growing light, Montana nodded. He spoke softly to Night Wolf in Shoshone.

Night Wolf answered, and he and Montana held a brief discussion in Shoshone.

Sergeant Mattern followed up immediately. 'Lieutenant, this here's Night Wolf. He's the chief warrior o' this here village. He's the feller I said I'd introduce ya to. Night Wolf, this here's Lieutenant Wilson.'

Night Wolf faced the young lieutenant and spoke in English. 'Lieutenant, you have come to my village like a coyote comes, when seeking to kill and run away. Why have you done this?'

Lieutenant Wilson drew himself up as if to snap to attention, then checked the impulse. He nodded his head at Night Wolf's words. 'I give you my apology, Night Wolf. I meant no disrespect to you or to your village. I am new in this country. I failed to understand that we should make noise to announce our presence and that we come in peace.'

'It is such an ignorance that causes unnecessary battles to be fought, and good men to die that should not have died that day.'

'I realize that, now. I did not know. I did not understand how keen the hearing of the Shoshone is, or how lightly you must sleep. It was my intention to announce our presence before we entered your village.'

'You and your men would have been sent to a different world before you set foot in our village.'

'I . . . I realize that now. Again, I give you my apology. I meant no harm.'

Night Wolf nodded as if satisfied. 'You have business that brings you here?'

'Yes, sir. Uh, I mean, yes. Yes, I do. I have been sent here by the United States Army to request your assistance, and, more specifically, the assistance of one Montana Keep.'

Montana grunted. 'Ain't nothin' the army wants what interests me one whit.'

Lieutenant Wilson swallowed hard, then plunged forward doggedly. 'Colonel Barker explained that you would almost certainly have misgivings about assisting the army in any way, at this time,' he acknowledged. 'He also asked me to express his profound sorrow and regret for the unnecessary loss of innocent civilian life incurred by his actions in the Logan's Creek affair. He admits to being somewhat out of control in anger over the atrocities visited upon his scout and your friend, Ian MacGreagor. In retrospect, he admits he should have handled that affair much differently, and taken precautions to protect the lives of the women and children involved.'

A long, pregnant silence enveloped the two groups, one still completely surrounded by the other. Incredulity gave a sharp edge to Montana's words. 'Ya mean he actually admits he done wrong?'

Lieutenant Wilson nodded vigorously. 'Yes, he does. In fact, he even sent a letter of regret for his actions to his own superiors, and offered to accept whatever discipline they were inclined to inflict upon him, including, if necessary, relief of his command.'

'He done that? On 'is own?'

The lieutenant nodded again. 'Yes, sir. He did. He seems genuinely penitent for that loss of life.'

'Well I'll be danged. Didn't figger thet blusterin' bag o' wind'd ever admit ta bein' wrong 'bout nothin'.'

Mattern interjected. 'Beggin' yer pardon, Lieutenant. Montana, if'n it makes any difference, ya got my word thet he means it. In all my years in this here man's army, I ain't never seen a officer apologize ta enlisted men. But Barker done made a speech ta the whole outfit, an' took the blame fer the whole shebang. Bawled when he did it, he did.'

Montana grunted again, obviously confused and affected by the old veteran's words.

Lieutenant Wilson took up the conversation. 'Be that as it may, Montana, the matter for which we were sent here is of some urgency. It is a matter of great importance not only to the army, but also to the Shoshone peoples. I ask if you would at least give me the opportunity to explain the situation, and relay the request with which I am charged to you.'

Montana grunted again, his brow furrowed in thought. After another long silence, he turned to Night Wolf and spoke in Shoshone.

Night Wolf nodded, turned, and spoke to the closest group of warriors. Instantly the circle of Shoshone warriors changed their stance, relaxing and lowering their weapons. One held his hands to his mouth and the sounds of night birds filled the air.

In response, leaves and branches began to rustle. In the gray light that heralds the sun's appearance, women and children materialized from nowhere, returning to the village. In minutes, fires were started and the smell of wood smoke grew tangy in the morning air.

Night Wolf addressed the lieutenant in English. 'You may tell your men to dismount and relax. They may make fires and fix food and eat. There is a stream a little ways over there, so they can care for their horses. You and your sergeant may accompany us to my village, and we will hear your words.'

'Thank you,' Lieutenant Wilson responded. He appeared to be about to say something further, but thought better of it and closed his mouth.

CHAPTER 13

'If it were any o' the Shoshone, Night Wolf'd know 'bout it.'

Lieutenant Wilson's eyebrows rose. 'You're absolutely certain of that?'

The young lieutenant scowled at Sergeant Mattern's snort of derision, but wisely decided not to challenge it.

The four men sat in a rough circle, just outside the Indian village, sitting cross-legged on the ground. Beyond them in the village, people went about their business, but cast frequent glances at the conference in progress that involved their leader. Montana's eyes twinkled briefly, before he said, 'Abs'lutely.'

'Then who do you think is behind it?'

Montana thought for a long moment. In the silence that ensued, Night Wolf spoke. 'It is not Indians.'

Wilson's head snapped up. 'What do you mean?

Who else would it be? There are signs of Indians at every scene.'

'Not Indian.' The chief warrior stared impassively then, and refused to speak further.

'How many's been hit?' Montana queried. 'All told.'

Wilson paused, visibly adding up in his mind. 'Six that I know of.'

'How many in each party?'

'The smallest was two. One wagon. Buggy, actually. The largest was a small wagon train, with four wagons. Seventeen souls. All dead. Scalped. Mutilated. Then burned with the remains of their wagons.'

'No survivors at all?'

'Just one.'

'Jist the kid?'

'Just him. Five years old, I think.'

'An' he said they was Indians?'

Wilson nodded. 'He was adamant about that. That's all we could get out of him, though. He'd just scream "Indians!" and then lapse into hysterics. Pitiful little fellow.'

'No survivors old enough to tell more?'

He shook his head. 'Not a one.'

'Nobody even managed ta sneak off inta the bushes er nothin'?'

'Nobody. Except the one child.'

'Who found him?'

'I did. I was leading a column, scouting for sign

of the marauders. We saw the smoke from the wagons, and rode to investigate. We found him standing in the open, sobbing, sucking on his thumb, staring at the burning remains of the wagon train.'

'Have a tracker with ya?'

'Only one of my men that does understand some rudiments of tracking. He confirmed that it was Indians, because none of the marauders' horses was shod.'

'Ya try ta foller 'em?'

'Of course. We were only able to do so for about a mile, before their trail was lost on hard ground and rocks.'

'An ever' time, they up an' collected the dead, heaped 'em inta the wagons, then burned 'em.'

Wilson nodded. 'They burned most of them. Not all. Those that weren't are how we know they raped, scalped and mutilated the victims.'

'Not Indian,' Night Wolf repeated.

Anger suffused Wilson's face momentarily, but he fought it down. 'Whether it is or not, it is certainly Indians who are getting the blame. Colonel Barker specifically requests your services, either as scout, or as leader of a unit of men, to pursue and identify the marauders. Once identified, the army will deal with them. You are not being asked to constitute a search and destroy unit.'

'Mighty consid'rate o' the army,' Montana observed.

'If you choose, you may also have any of your, ah, Indian, ah, friends accompany you.'

'Ya mean I kin take a coupla warriors with us?'

'If you choose, as many as you wish, you may do so.'

Montana lifted his brows, looking at Night Wolf. He spoke to him in Shoshone. Night Wolf stared hard at Montana for several heartbeats, then at the lieutenant. Then he answered, also speaking in Shoshone, and speaking at length.

Montana answered, and the two conversed for several minutes. When silence fell between them for several minutes more, Montana took a deep breath. 'I s'pect they ain't no way o' findin' out who's doin' it, 'cept to find out who's doin' it. Kin I pick the men I want?'

Lieutenant Wilson considered for a long moment before he said, 'Yes.'

'Then I want Mattern, Will Steiger, Ansel Ferguson, an' two Shoshone o' Night Wolf's choosin', besides him.'

'Good choices,' Mattern approved.

Wilson nodded. 'They are my best three men. That will leave me rather vulnerable in returning to Fort Fetterman, but I said you could pick. I will stand by my word.'

Without another word, Montana and Night Wolf rose and walked away. Lieutenant Wilson, obviously nonplussed by their abrupt departure, looked inquiringly at Sergeant Mattern. Ford nodded his head toward where the rest of their unit waited, then he stood, hesitating long enough that he and the lieutenant stood together. When they were out of earshot, Lieutenant Wilson asked, 'What happens now?'

Mattern explained, 'Wal, us three fella's gotta get ready ta ride. The rest o' the unit needs ta leave now, an' head back ta the fort. When they's ready, Montana an' the others'll jist ride out, an' figger we'll fall in.'

Wilson shook his head. 'I do not understand people in this country.'

Mattern grinned. 'Ye're learnin'. Doin' a right smart job of it, matter o' fact.'

Wilson acted as if he were going to stop and throw his arms around the grizzled sergeant, before his military training snapped him back into a stiff march toward his men.

Montana was having a much more difficult time of things in his own tepee. Rain Crow stood to one side, watching, her bemusement obvious on her face, but saying nothing. It was Laura who was his biggest problem at the moment.

Laura faced Montana squarely, arms folded across her chest. 'Don't you understand?' she demanded of him. 'It's Two Feathers! All he's waiting for, is for you to leave the village. Then he'll come charging in with a bunch of his braves to recapture me. They're killing all those people, knowing you will be the one the army calls on to find them.'

'He's had 'nough time ta do all that,' Montana conceded. 'But they ain't no part of it what sounds like nothin' Two Feathers'd do. It's too far-fetched, ta think he'd spend all thet thar time an' lay all them ambushes, jist ta git me ta leave this here village.'

'You don't know Two Feathers. You don't know how badly he wants me. It's him, I'm telling you.'

'Wal, if 'n it is, I'll figger it out soon enough, an' come a-hightailin' it back here.'

'Then it will be too late, and I'll be gone.'

'There'll be enough warriors here ta pertect the village. They's only three a-goin'.'

'Besides me. I'm going too.'

'What?'

'I said I'm going too. I am not staying here, waiting helplessly to be victimized yet again. Give me a gun and a horse. I'll keep up, and I can shoot with the best of them.'

Montana shook his head decisively. 'Ain't fittin' ta have a woman along on a caper like this'un.'

'Neither is it fitting to leave an unwilling woman here who does not wish to be left behind. Besides, I, I. . . .'

All at once the defiance melted away, and she seemed to shrink back into herself. Fighting back tears, she glanced at Rain Crow, then looked imploringly at Montana. 'It . . . it's not just that. I . . . I just can't. I absolutely can't! I can't bear the thought of staying here as the only white woman in an Indian village again. I know these are your friends, and I know Rain Crow is your wife, but. . . .'

'You're plumb safe here.'

'I can't. I'm sorry. I absolutely cannot. I cannot make myself stay here alone. If you will not allow me to accompany you, then I will flee at once, and try to make my own way to Fort Fetterman, or wherever there are white people.'

'Now see here, woman! Ya can't go galavantin' off 'cross the country all by yerself! Why, if Two Feathers is out a-lookin' fer ya, he'll have ya quicker'n a frog snaggin' a fly outa the air with 'is tongue.'

'Nevertheless, that is exactly what I shall be forced to do, if I am not allowed to accompany you.'

Montana turned to his wife, his eyes pleading for help. She spoke to him in Shoshone. He answered sharply, anger tingeing his voice. Rain Crow looked down, but her words were firm as she responded. Their conversation continued several minutes, then lapsed into silence.

Angrily, Montana threw up his hands. 'Have it your way, then. But mind, we ain't holdin' back none on account o' you bein' a woman. Keep up or git left behind by yerself.'

He wheeled and lunged from the tepee, muttering under his breath, 'An' only one of 'em's my wife. An' some o' these folks got two er three of 'em! What in the world a man wants with more'n one is beyond me. Takin' a woman along huntin' a war party! Givin' in, jist 'cause my woman says I gotta. Oughta jist head out ta the mountains alone, that's what I oughta do. Do as I dang please then. Tell the army where ta go too. Let 'em do their own varmint huntin'. See how well they do then. Bull-headed woman'd do it too. Take right off by 'erself an' walk right smack inta Two Feathers afore she got ten miles. Serve 'er right, too, it would. Oughta jist let 'er do it, that's what I oughta do.'

His quiet tirade was interrupted by Night Wolf. 'Does my friend have trouble?'

'We all got trouble,' Montana gritted. 'Danged wisp of a girl's goin' along.'

Night Wolf's surprise was etched across his face. 'You will take the young woman with you?'

'I reckon.'

'She is your new wife?'

'No, she ain't no wife o' mine. Jist askeert o' stayin' here without me a-bein' here.'

Understanding replaced the surprise on the warrior's face. 'She feels safe with you.'

'Somethin' like that.'

Night Wolf nodded. 'If she were my woman, I would like for her to be protected by you.'

'This here ain't no pertectin' caper. This here's a hunt fer a war party.'

'Not Indians.'

123

'Yeah, I heerd ya say somethin' 'bout thet. How's come yer so sure?'

Night Wolf shrugged. 'It does not feel like a thing done by Indians.'

'Well, we'll find out.'

'I have sent youngsters to bring your horse and your pack horse. I will send one to get another horse for the white woman.'

'Wouldn't happen ta have a white man's saddle lyin' around somewhere too, that she could use, would ya?'

Night Wolf smiled for the first time Montana could remember. 'It is an army saddle.'

Montana started to ask the obvious, then thought better of it. 'It'll have ta do.'

An hour later, four white men, three Shoshone warriors, and one white woman with flaming red hair rode out. One of the soldiers, now dressed at Montana's command in civilian clothing, held the lead rope of a heavily laden pack horse.

CHAPTER 14

'Worse'n anythin' I ever seen,' Sergeant Ford Mattern growled.

Montana nodded, his lips compressed to a thin straight line.

The three Shoshone warriors sat their horses, impassive, staring as if unmoved by the scene. Montana knew them well enough, however, to note the stiffness of their shoulders, the lift of their chins, the narrowing of their eyes. They were as moved as the soldiers by the scene, but too disciplined to let it show.

The other two soldiers had no such ability. Both Corporal Ferguson and Will Steiger had taken one look, then tumbled from their saddles, bending over to throw up violently on the ground. Ansel Ferguson recovered quickly, then moved to divert Laura from the scene of carnage. She had already seen enough. She allowed the solicitous soldier to put an arm around her shoulders and lead her away, seating her on a large rock, facing away from the object of their discomfiture. He handed her his canteen. Her eyes expressed her gratitude as she removed the lid and took a long drink.

Without their seeming to realize it, over the five days since they had left the Shoshone village, Laura had begun to keep close to Montana less and less. Slowly she had begun to ride beside Corporal Ferguson instead, seeming to prefer the more talkative company of his presence. He, in turn, had become more and more solicitous of her, even placing himself where he could protect her privacy when she needed to retreat into some clump of brush to relieve herself.

He hovered close to her now, watching her carefully, as the rest looked over the remnants of what had been four immigrant wagons.

It was a horrifyingly grisly scene. Half-burned bodies were draped over the remains of burned out wagons. The shattered head of a small child was caught in the steel spokes of a wagon wheel, whose wood had burned away. It was a slight, blonde girl, perhaps seven or eight years old. Half her hair was burned away, and one side of her face was blackened. A hole in the top of her head bore silent testimony to her cause of death. Much of the skull was caved in there, leaving bloody brain tissue visible within. It was the sight of her, and the smell of burned flesh, more than the rest of the carnage, that had sickened even the seasoned veterans.

Every occupant of the small wagon train was dead. What was left of their charred corpses was scalped and mutilated. Half a dozen arrows jutted from the dead, or from sides of wagons.

Montana approached one such arrow, studying it carefully.

'See somethin'?' Sergeant Mattern queried.

'What d'ya make o' thet?' Montana asked, rather than answer the question.

'Nothin' outa the ordinary, I guess,' Mattern hesitated. 'Jist a stray arrer.'

'But the wagon box is pretty well burned.'

'Yep. So's the rest of 'em.'

'But the arrer ain't.'

Mattern's eyes opened a bit wider. 'Huh! Thet's funny. You'da thought it'd burn along with all t'other stuff.'

'Let's look at t'others.'

Gingerly they stepped around pieces of still smoldering remains. They examined an arrow protruding from the side of one body. 'Thet thar's Pawnee,' Montana observed, pointing out the fletching on the arrow.

'Shore 'nuff is,' Mattern agreed. 'The other'n wasn't.'

'It was Absarack, looked like.'

'Thet or Lakota.'

'Let's check out thet spear.'

They made their way to the feathered spear jutting from the back of a woman's unburned

127

corpse. 'Now thet thar don't make no sense at all,' Montana growled.

'Ain't no Arapaho in the country, far's I know,' Mattern agreed.

'Not Indians,' Night Wolf spoke from Montana's elbow.

'Seems to be,' Mattern argued.

'Too many different,' Night Wolf insisted.

'He's right,' Montana agreed. 'Every arrer an' spear we've found is from some diff'rent tribe. They ain't no way thet many diff'rent tribes'd be runnin' together, attackin' folks.'

'Bunch o' renegades,' Mattern offered. 'Outcasts from their own people, banded together, raisin' havoc, runnin' amok.'

'Could be,' Montana agreed. 'Seems odd nobody's noticed 'em, if'n thet's the case.'

'That might be because everyone that's seen them is dead,' Mattern pointed out.

Will Steiger chose that time to ride up to the three. 'Shore 'nuff Indians, all raght,' he drawled.

'Howd'ya know?' Montana challenged.

'Just from the tracks,' Steiger explained. 'All the shod tracks are animals from the wagon train what didn't get kilt. They ran them all off with 'em when they left. But their tracks coming and waiting ain't shod. Nary one shod horse among 'em. Only Indians ride unshod horses.'

'Well, thet's true 'nuff,' Montana admitted. 'Still don't smell right.'

'Not Indians,' Night Wolf repeated stubbornly.

'Tell me why'n thunder it ain't,' Mattern challenged.

Montana translated the sergeant's demand into Shoshone, even though he well knew Night Wolf understood every word the soldier said.

'They do not act like any Indian would act,' Night Wolf explained in Shoshone, waiting for Montana to translate, then continued.

'Indians would not drag the bodies to where they could burn them. That is too much an act of respect of the dead, and they do not respect their enemies. If it was a noble warrior they had killed, some might, but they would then be certain to burn them completely, or to build a burial platform for them. These are half burned in carelessness, to make them look and smell bad. It is not a thing any Indian would have a reason to do.'

When Montana had translated the longest speech the Shoshone warrior had made since leaving his village, Mattern pursed his lips thoughtfully. 'Well, kin we follow the tracks?'

'We kin foller 'em,' Montana assured him.

They did so, following carefully, with Montana remaining 300 yards ahead of the rest, lest the whole party be led into a trap.

When night fell, they camped near a seep spring, cared for their horses, and rolled into their bed rolls.

Montana noted with approval that Corporal

Ferguson spread his own bed roll between Laura's and the rest of the men's, considerably closer to hers than theirs. 'Keepin' a purty good eye on 'er,' he muttered.

The third day following the trail Montana held up his hand, halting the group trailing well back from him. He dismounted and walked around a large depression, studying the ground carefully. Then he climbed the sides of the hollow, studying the ground on both sides. After a few minutes, the rest of the group dismounted and allowed their horses to rest and crop grass from the tall growth that grew lush in the whole valley.

Finally, when he had carefully gone over the whole area, Montana rejoined them.

'Dangest thing I ever seen,' he announced.

'Whatd'ya find?' Mattern demanded.

'The bunch we been a-follerin' stumbled on to someone. Indians, too, 'pears to be. Got set afore the new ones rode inta the holler. Opened up on 'em, an' kilt the whole bunch.'

'I could see a couple horses from here.' Will Steiger interjected.

Montana nodded. 'They's three. Three horses got kilt, an' lay whar they fell. They ain't nothin' else there, 'ceptin' tracks an' sign. Lots o' blood on the ground an' grass an' all.'

'No bodies?'

'Nary a one.'

'Any sign of 'em bein' buried?'

'Nope.'

The group looked at one another in confusion. It was Laura who voiced the question in everyone's mind. 'Why in the world would anyone kill a bunch of people, then haul their bodies away?'

They all looked at each other again, and every stare was returned as blankly as the one received.

'I ain't never heard o' such a thing,' Sergeant Mattern said finally. 'Folks are likely to carry off their own dead an' wounded. Never heard o' carryin' off others. What do they want with them dead bodies? You sure they was all dead?'

Montana shrugged. 'Cain't be sure. Most of 'em's gotta be, though. Too much blood ever'where.'

'How long ago?' Steiger queried.

'Couple days. Blood's good'n black. Flies blowed the deep puddles of it a'ready.'

'Where'd they go?'

'Rode off thataway. Looked like most of 'em was leadin' a horse, an' they was drivin' the other horses an' cattle what they took off'n thet wagon train.'

'Headin' for somewhere,' Mattern observed.

Montana nodded. 'Looks like they most likely stumbled onta this bunch o' Indians, got the drop on 'em, an' jist wiped 'em out.'

'But why'n thunder'd they take the bodies?' Mattern asked again.

Nobody answered. Finally, the sergeant said,

'Well, it's gettin' on today. We'd as well find a spot to camp. Follow 'em tomorrow.'

As they pitched camp this time, Montana noted that Laura and Ferguson placed their bed rolls right next to each other, again away from the rest of the group. It did not escape his notice that she seemed less and less to care where he was, so long as Ferguson was close. He felt a sudden pang of emotion he didn't understand, and fought down a feeling of emptiness that suddenly surged within him. Scowling, he turned his attention to getting the group fed and bedded down for the night.

First light saw them all in the saddle again. It was scarcely past midmorning when another scene of carnage appeared before them.

This time neither the wagon nor any bodies were burned. Two couples, obviously traveling together, had been ambushed from cover. In spite of being caught by surprise, they had fought valiantly. Seven Indians lay dead in a circle around the two wagons. The wagons had been ransacked. False bottoms had been discovered and emptied in both wagons. Otherwise, the victims lay where they had fallen. Two had arrows jutting from their bodies. The others had multiple gunshot wounds. The women had obviously been brutally raped before being killed.

Montana had again halted the others while he surveyed the scene, then motioned for them to join him. He did not miss Laura's reaction. A small gasp escaped from her lips. She rode close to Corporal Ferguson, grabbing his arm, saying something to him. They were close enough for Montana to hear his answer, even though he hadn't heard what Laura said.

'You sure?' Ferguson asked.

Laura only nodded, gripping the corporal's arm tighter. She pointed with the hand that held her reins, at one of the bodies on the ground.

'What is it?' Montana demanded.

'She says that Indian lying over there looks like Two Feathers.'

Just then Night Wolf joined them, pulling his horse to a stop beside them. 'Absaroka,' he announced. 'War party. They came to search for the woman.'

'How kin ya tell thet?' Montana demanded.

'No other reason seven Absaroka would be in Shoshone land.'

Montana thought it over for a long moment, frowning. 'Wal, they's Absaraks, all right. They warn't kilt here, though.'

'They weren't?' Laura demanded at once.

'Nope. No blood on the ground around 'em at all. They is from the folks in the wagons. The Indians is all ones what was kilt back yonder in thet holler, then hauled here.'

'Arrows shot into dead white men,' Night Wolf offered.

'What?'

'Men already dead when arrows shot into them,' Night Wolf repeated. 'No blood around arrows. Arrow wound bleeds much. No blood. Absaroka not kill people.'

'This whole mess just gets more and more confusing,' Will Steiger offered.

'Gettin' clearer,' Montana disagreed.

'You got it figgered out?' Mattern demanded.

'Not fer sure,' Montana evaded. 'Near, but not fer sure.'

Laura continued to stare at the body of Two Feathers, a strange mixture of relief and grief etched on to her features. Finally she said, 'I want to bury him.'

'What?'

'I want to bury Two Feathers.'

'Let the coyotes eat 'im,' Mattern growled.

Corporal Ferguson, studying Laura intently, asked softly, 'Why do you want to bury him, Laura?'

She shuddered, then took a deep breath and lifted her chin. 'He loved me,' she said simply.

Ferguson studied her face for a long moment, then nodded. 'Would you order a burial detail, Sergeant? We need to bury the white folks anyway. It won't hurt anything to bury the Indian too.'

'Not in the same grave, we hain't,' Steiger said with surprising intensity.

'Don't have to be in the same grave. I think she just wants to be very sure he's dead, and she did obviously have some feelings for him, even though she was his prisoner. As she said, he loved her.'

Whatever answer Steiger offered was lost to incoherent mumblings as he stomped away to begin the unpleasant duty.

CHAPTER 15

The sun bore down with the intensity of high altitude and sparse humidity. It sucked the moisture from any square inch of exposed skin, burning it dark and leathery. It used up the body's store of liquid, leaving mouths feeling as if filled with cotton. It assaulted eyes, making them squint and pull the brows downward, craving even the scant shade they provided. It puckered lines into the corners of eyes, giving those too long exposed a premature wrinkled appearance.

The only ones the sun and heat didn't seem to bother were the three Shoshone warriors. They bore it with the same stoic acceptance with which they met the rest of habitually hard lives.

Montana's squinting eyes peered out from beneath the brim of the old slouch hat, ragged at the edges, stained by gallons of sweat and endless dust.

Beside him the Shoshone warriors ranged, each

watching the scene below. The rest of the company was back a little way, below the brow of the hill, lest too many eyes cause their position to be discovered.

'The one thet worries me most is the one what cut off by hisself,' Montana muttered.

Behind him, but well within hearing, Sergeant Mattern responded, 'Where ya reckon 'e was goin'?'

'If'n I knowed, I wouldn't be worryin' 'bout 'im.'

An Indian spoke softly, pointing with an arm kept carefully below the rim of the ridge. Following his gesture, Montana turned his head and grunted. 'Someone comin' fer a fact. Ever'body keep yer head down. Whoever it is ain't in no hurry, but we don't want 'em spottin' us.'

Below them, beyond the rim of the ridge behind which they kept carefully concealed, a sprawling ranch yard sweltered in the sun. The corral was nearly full of horses. Others grazed nearby, kept close by hobbles. Numerous cattle dotted the valley whose view the ranch yard commanded.

Their vantage point provided a full view of the yard and corrals, as well as the road approaching the ranch. So far they had seen little activity. From time to time someone had come from the house to the barn and back again. Occasionally a man would leave the house, visit the outhouse, then return to the house. Otherwise there was little to watch.

'Buggies,' Will Steiger said suddenly. 'It looks like three buggies.'

'Now who'd be comin' out here in fancy buggies?'

They watched in crouched silence, peering through bushes and sage brush, as the procession of buggies, led by a lone horseman, came nearer and nearer.

'Looks like all women,' Ansel Ferguson noted.

'Fancy dressed ones,' Matters agreed.

'Whores!' Steiger drawled. 'Them's the whores from the hog ranch.'

'You'd know,' Mattern muttered.

'What're the whores from the hog ranch doin' clear out here?' Steiger continued, as if he hadn't been interrupted. 'It's a hard day's trip by buggy from there ta here.'

'Well, I 'spect we know where the other rider cut off to,' Mattern surmised, 'but how'd they talk all the ladies from the hog ranch ta come clear out here? An' what fer?'

'That's a stupid question if I ever heard one,' Laura responded, her voice edged and brittle. 'What do those kind of women always want. Money. Money and a good time. Someone has an awfully lot of money. Money enough to make it worth their while for that many of them to spend all that time coming out here and going back.'

'Looks like they're fixin' ta have a lulu of a shindig, all right,' Steiger offered. His voice had none of the brittle hardness of Laura's, only a tinge of wishfulness.

'So what d'we do now?' Sergeant Mattern cut in.

'Nothin,' Montana muttered.

'Nothin'?'

'Nothin'. Fer now. Settle down an' git some rest. Find yerselves a nice shady spot. Take a nap. We'll jist wait till pertneart sundown, then we'll mosey down an' have a look around. Once the party gits goin', they ain't likely ta have no lookouts, an' nobody payin' a whole lot o' 'tention ta nothin' 'cept them women an' them cases o' whiskey they're haulin' inta the house.'

Ansel and Laura moved off at once to a large clump of buck brush, nearly ten feet tall. They sat down together in its shade, talking quietly.

The others found whatever spot of shade they could, drank from canteens, and lay back on the warm ground. Most covered their face with their hats.

The three Shoshone warriors simply stretched out where they were and continued to watch the ranch yard.

Inch by inch the broiling sun crept toward the western horizon. As the shadows began to lengthen, Montana crawled back to the lip of the ridge.

In Shoshone he asked Night Wolf, 'Has anything changed?'

'It seems a time to have sport. Much whiskey.

Someone makes music on the box that is rubbed with a stick sometimes, and people yell a lot. No lookouts.'

Montana nodded. 'Well, let's slip down an' have a look-see.'

Summoning the others in whispered tones, Montana assigned details. 'Ferguson, stay up here an' keep watch so's nothin' happens ta Laura.'

He didn't miss the look that passed back and forth between them, but he ignored it, moving quickly to the others. 'Runs Plenty, you'n Steiger move round thataway an' come at the house straight past the outhouse. Night Wolf, you'n Afraid Of Fox circle way round an' make sure nobody gits up thet draw behind the house. If'n men come thataway, shoot 'em. If'n any o' them women do, shoo 'em back ta the house an' tell 'em ta lie flat an' stay put. All o' ya, if'n it comes ta a fight, which I'm bettin' it will, don't go shootin' low. They'll be womenfolk lyin' on the floor, an' we don't wanta be hittin' them.'

'It would certainly be no loss,' Laura snapped.

Will Steiger could hold his tongue no longer. 'Fer someone jist as much despised as them whores by most folks, ya sure ain't got no compassion. Ya sound jist like them ol' biddies that'd say the very same thing about you.'

The words were scarcely out of his mouth before Ansel Ferguson's fist connected with his chin, sending him sprawling on the ground.

He came to his feet cursing and lunged head-long into the other soldier, sending him reeling backward. They both went to the ground in a tangle, fists, knees, elbows, feet and foreheads lashing out at each other.

Sergeant Mattern and Montana hurried forward, grabbing the pair and dragging them backward, away from each other.

'Corporal,' Mattern snapped at Ferguson, 'You are an officer. I expect more rational behavior than that from you.'

'How 'bout him?' Ferguson demanded. 'Did you hear what he called Laura. He said she wasn't no better'n—'

'I heard what he said,' Mattern interrupted. He turned toward Laura. 'And a good part of what he said is fair and true. You, of all people, ought to be a whole lot less quick to look down yer nose at other wimin.'

'Yeah, see?' Steiger demanded.

Mattern wheeled toward him, sending him staggering with a looping right to the side of the head, followed by a jabbing finger. In a blistering tone, he managed somehow to yell at a whisper, 'An' you kin keep yer mouth shut, Private, er ya'll be in the stockade when we git back ta Fetterman. Y'understand?'

Steiger opened his mouth to argue, then his training abruptly caught up to him. He snapped to attention, saluted, and in a quiet voice that dripped with tension and anger gritted, 'Yes, sir!'

'Then don't fergit it, or I'll have Runs Plenty leave ya head first in the outhouse on yer way by it.'

The Shoshone warrior, who had, up to that point, given no indication of understanding English, chuckled unexpectedly.

Mattern wheeled back to the others. 'Now ever'-body git whar yer s'posed ta be, an' make it quick. Ya got fifteen minutes, then we move in. No shootin', 'less ya gotta, 'til me or Montana opens the show.'

His glare daring anyone to disagree or prolong the confrontation, he stood with his hands on his hips. There was no hesitation. Everyone moved quickly and quietly to his assigned station.

When the fifteen minutes had elapsed, Mattern addressed Corporal Ferguson. 'Corporal, keep your eyes peeled. If anyone comes up the road, find a way to let us know. Otherwise, be sure nobody escapes this way, and take care of the woman.'

'I give 'er one o' my guns,' Ferguson said.

'Ya what?'

'I give 'er one o' my guns,' he repeated.

Laura held up a rifle nobody had noticed in her hand before. 'I can shoot very well,' she said, her words pronounced carefully and archly.

A long silence hung heavily in the gathering dusk, as Mattern and Montana glared at the pair in turn. Finally Mattern shrugged. 'Jist be danged sure what yer shootin',' he said as he wheeled away.

Even in the dimming light, the angry reddening of both her face and that of Ferguson was obvious, but neither the grizzled veteran nor the seasoned mountain man chose to acknowledge it. In a little better light, the small smile on Montana's face may have been noticed, however.

CHAPTER 16

'Not a shod horse in the bunch,' Mattern whispered.

Montana nodded. 'But the saddles an' stuff in there's all cowboy stuff. Thet ain't all what's there, though.'

'What else ya find?'

Sergeant Mattern had moved slowly and quietly through the corral, checking the horses, while Montana moved into the deeper gloom of the shed that passed for a barn, checking on its contents.

'Lots o' Indian stuff.'

'Indian stuff?'

'Yep. Bows an' arrers. Sev'ral spears. Head bands. Couple o' breech-clouts. A roach.'

'Stuff they took off'n them dead Indians?'

'Them an' a bunch o' others, looks like. Dark. Couldn't tell fer sure. Danged if'n some don't look

144

like Pawnee stuff. Some Cheyenne. Some looks like 'Rapaho, but it's too dark to tell fer sure.'

'So it's them been doin' it all, an' blamin' it on Indians.'

'Yep. Looks like. How we gonna do this here?'

A long pause indicated the seasoned veteran had also been mulling the problem over in his own mind. Sounds of revelry rocked steadily from the house. Even so, they both well knew these were experienced, hardened outlaws, who would react swiftly and violently when threatened.

'Whilst yer a-thinkin',' Montana whispered, 'I 'spect I'll see if'n I kin git all the horses outa the c'ral an' scattered, without them a-hearin' nothin'.'

Mattern nodded. 'That'll maybe keep any of 'em from gittin' away from us,' he agreed.

Moving slowly and quietly, crooning softly to the horses, Montana opened the gate and allowed the animals to leave. As soon as they saw the door to freedom stood wide open before them, they lost no time availing themselves of the opportunity. One lone mottled grey gelding remained, standing against the corral fence, holding one leg so no weight rested on it.

'Got a lame one,' Montana observed. 'An' jist left 'im be, looks like. Wal, t'ain't nobody goin' nowheres on him. We'll tend ta him later.'

When he moved back beside Sergeant Mattern, the soldier was ready with a plan. 'If we just let 'em know we're here, they'll hunker down an' we'll have a three-day battle. Some o' us, and fer sure some o' the whores'll get shot up, along with 'em.'

'They kin hold us off fer 'bout as long as they want in there,' Montana agreed. 'It's a well-built house.'

'Yeah. But I can see two lamps, a-sittin' on the table. They'll be lightin' 'em any minit. If we shoot both lamps out, one of 'em's sure ta start a fire. They can't fight the fires without makin' themselves purty good targets for us. They'll most likely come out in a rush, shootin' an' shoutin'.'

'What about the wimin?'

'That's the problem. Without the fire, they're all smart enough ta hit the floor an' stay low. But if we set the house afire, they got nowheres ta go other than outside, where all the bullets is gonna be flyin'.'

Just then a man and woman came out the front door. He had an arm around her waist, a bottle of whiskey in his other hand, and was nuzzling her ear as they walked. 'Headin' fer a private spot,' Montana whispered.

'If we move now, they'll spot us sure,' Mattern agreed.

'Sure hope he's thinkin' hard 'nough 'bout certain parts o' her body he don't notice the horses is gone,' Montana whispered back.

The two moved together to a patch of soft-looking grass, clearly visible to the watching eyes in the

146

ghostly light of the full moon, just rising above the horizon.

'Stay put,' Montana disappeared.

The words were no sooner out of his mouth than he disappeared as completely as though he were an apparition suddenly dissolving into nothingness. As Mattern watched, he appeared again, just at the feet of the couple, enthralled in their pleasures on the ground.

Neither of them was aware of his presence until Montana's gun barrel cracked against the man's skull with a thunk Mattern could clearly hear from the edge of the corral.

The man collapsed on to the woman, pinning her effectively to the ground. Montana swiftly clamped a hand over her mouth, and knelt beside her.

Speaking in an urgent whisper, he said, 'Hold still an' listen, woman!'

Her eyes, wide with terror, cast about wildly before slowing and fixing their gaze on Montana's face. 'If'n I move my hand, ya gonna keep quiet?' he demanded.

After only an instant, she nodded. He moved his hand instantly. 'Listen quick'n hard,' his urgent whisper demanded. 'All hell's gonna bust loose in 'bout five minutes. These here fellas is the ones what been-a slaughterin' folks an' blamin' it on Indians. Git the word ta t'other wimin quick's ya can, without spillin' no beans. When the shootin' starts, all of ya head out the front door fast, an' run straight ta the corral. We'll be 'spectin' ya.'

She digested the information instantly. 'Why can't we just lie on the floor until it's over? We should be safe there, and they won't think we're the ones that told you where they are.'

'Cuz we're gonna smoke 'em out. Only way we can 'void a three-day battle is commence by shootin' out the lamps. Thet'll set fire ta the house, sure's sunup.'

'How long do I have?'

'We'll give ya five minutes.'

'Can you make it ten? I'll have to have time to talk with all of them without it being obvious.'

Montana visibly debated with himself for several seconds. 'Ya got ten,' he agreed then. 'No more.'

'Then get this hulk off of me, so I can get up.'

'Done a'ready, is he?'

Her eyes went flat and hard. 'Don't get smart.'

'If'n I was smart, I wouldn't tip our hand this-away.'

Her glare softened as he rolled the unconscious Lothario off her, allowing her to rise. 'I do appreciate that,' she whispered. 'All the girls will. Thank you.'

Ignoring her words he said, 'When ya git to the c'ral, hunker down inside it an' wait till the festivities is quieted down. Then we'll round up yer horses an' hitch up your buggies.'

'Thank you,' she said again, as she moved toward

the house. By the time she reached the front door, Montana had again disappeared.

As the woman stepped through the door, a voice called out, 'Where's Clancy?'

'Passed out drunk,' she responded. The hard edge of derision in her voice made her words totally convincing. She added, 'Lot of fun he was.'

The bodiless voice rejoined, 'Well, let's me'n you wander back out there. I'm bettin' I can do a whole lot better job.'

Her voice took on a teasing and flirting tone instantly. 'Now that sounds like the best offer I've had all night. Give me a minute to share something with the other girls, then we'll go see if you're as much man as you think you are.'

'Ya best tell 'em what ya wanta tell 'em now, then,' he responded. 'Cuz you' n me's gonna be outside for a long while!'

As though sharing some choice bit of gossip about her supposedly passed out paramour, she called a pair of whores who were fussing over one of the outlaws. One of them kissed him on the ear and said, 'Don't go anywhere, honey. We'll be right back.'

He patted one of them on the rear as they moved away to hear what the other said to them. On cue, they giggled as if the anecdote she related were particularly funny. Each, in turned, rushed off to share it with others. In less than five minutes, the supposed tidbit had been shared with every one of them.

It seemed almost as if such a scenario had been rehearsed among them. Talking and giggling like schoolgirls, they began to bunch together, moving unnoticed closer to the front door as they did so.

One of the outlaws called out, 'Hey, you ladies didn't come out here to yak'n giggle with one another. Git over here'n remind me what I been a-missin' so long.'

The woman who had been drinking with him turned and made a kissing face at him, then smiled, 'Keep your pants on, sweetheart. I'll be right back.'

'I ain't keepin' 'em on much longer,' he shot back. 'We didn't bring ya'll out here to be fittin' an' proper ya know.'

The object of his desires made another flirting face at him. 'Don't worry, cowboy. I'm worth the wait.'

'Ya better be! It's been a long wait, I'm tellin' ya.'

Outside, each crouched behind a large post of the corral, Mattern whispered to Montana. 'Ready?'

'All set. Jist give the word.'

'On three, then. One, two—'

The word three was drowned out by two rifles barking as one. Two freshly lit lamps in the house shattered, exploding coal oil and fire across the dry wooden tables, and on to the curtains of one of the windows. The flames began to spread immediately.

Pandemonium broke loose inside the house. Almost instantly guns fired, sending bullets screaming blindly out through the windows. The front door flew open. The women erupted through it, running headlong in a bunch for the corral.

The last woman was scarcely through the door before a man stepped into it. Cursing violently, the same voice they had heard before yelled, 'They set us up! The whores set us up!'

He raised a gun and fired into the fleeing backs of the women. One of them threw up her arms and fell headlong on the ground. Two rifles from the corral responded instantly to the perfect target, framed in the doorway, illuminated by the quickly expanding flames behind him. He went down in a crumpled heap without a sound.

Two of the women stopped to try to help the fallen one, while the rest rushed into the corral, crouching and lying on the ground at the center of the enclosure, making themselves as small as possible.

The two who had stopped quickly realized their companion was dead. They swiftly abandoned her body to join the rest in the corral.

A steady hail of gunfire roared from the house, answered by fire from the surrounding cover on all sides.

Abruptly the outlaws broke from the burning house in a rush, exiting through both front and back doors, and crashing through windows.

Clear targets in the light of the full moon, as well as that of the fire, they stood no chance. Most of them made it only a few steps before being cut down by the lethal accuracy of the withering fire from the surrounding brush.

Only one, running fast, bent low and dodging from side to side, managed to dive into the brush almost exactly between the closest of the sources of fire directed at the house.

'See thet'un?' Montana grunted.

'Seen 'im.' Mattern responded. 'Couldn't get a bead on 'im.'

'I'll chase 'im down.'

Mattern only nodded, watching for any indication of other survivors. Behind the bodies strewn in the yard, the ranch house quickly became a monstrous pyre, shooting flames fifty feet into the air.

CHAPTER 17

He was clear of the circle of attackers. Two pistols tucked into his waistband, a rifle in each hand, and two belts of ammunition slung over his shoulders, he was confident now. He had noted the direction of the tracks of several horses, and recognized those of his favorite mount. If he could get within calling distance, he knew he could call the animal to him, and he would be mounted and away.

With all the rest dead, as they surely were, there was nobody alive who knew who had masterminded the idea. When things quieted down, he had enough ill-gotten booty stashed to live in style for many years.

The whores had seen him, but he was positive none of them knew his name. Nor would they see him again, to identify him. He would never sully himself by actually touching such a woman. Besides, for all they knew, he was dead along with the others. With the ranch house burning as it was, they would never know how many bodies were completely cremated within it.

His biggest regret was that now the whole country would know it wasn't Indians wreaking the violent depredations on hapless and helpless victims around the country. That severely lessened the likelihood of accomplishing his primary goal.

After all, he didn't really need the money. The raping and killing had been fun, he had to admit. It had given him a rush of exhilaration he'd never felt in his life. But he'd have to do without that, now. At least, for the time being.

He almost chuckled as he congratulated himself on his cleverness and the good fortune of his escape, unscathed, from what had become a perfect trap.

'Hold it right there!'

Panic leaped into his throat and rushed through him. It was followed instantly by a chill that felt as if his heart had stopped. That, in turn, was replaced at once by a red surge of anger.

The rifle in his right hand swung to cover the spot from which the voice had emanated. 'Who's there?' he demanded.

'Drop the guns,' was the answer, instead of an explanation.

Another voice, transmitting astonishment, cried out, 'David?'

'You know him?' the first voice responded.

Unbelief tinged the outlaw's voice as he

answered, 'Laura? Is that you, Laura?'

'David! What are you doing here?'

'What are you doing here?' he responded, rather than answer.

Her voice grew instantly hard and cold. 'That's neither here nor there. Why are you here? Why were you with those outlaws in that house?'

Silence prevailed for several seconds. Both Laura and the man with her stepped from the cover of the brush, facing David across twenty feet of buffalo grass. She repeated her question. 'Why are you here with them, David?'

He chuckled suddenly. 'Who do you think figured out this whole plan?' His answer was more of a boast than a question.

'You planned all those terrible things they've been doing?'

'Who else would've ever thought of it?'

'Who is this guy?' the man with Laura demanded again.

Laura took a long breath. 'Ansel, this is my brother. David Cunningham.'

'Your brother?' Ansel demanded. 'The one that tried to kill you?'

'One and the same,' she confirmed.

Even in the softening glow of the moonlight, his glare was hard and brittle. 'I'd have succeeded, too, if it wasn't for that interfering idiot of a mountain man.'

'I'm sure you would have,' she agreed. 'He saved

my life three times. Once from the Indians, and twice from you.'

'I'd have saved you from the Indians,' he protested.

'By killing me,' she shot back. 'Some way to save your sister!'

'What choice did I have?' he argued. 'You was already ruined. No decent white man would ever have you after being some savage buck's squaw. By now I suppose you couldn't even be satisfied with anyone but a stinking Indian.'

'I'd have her, and plumb proud,' Ansel inserted.

'Who are you?' David demanded.

'Name's Ansel Ferguson,' Ansel responded. 'The man who intends to be Laura's husband.'

'Husband!' David echoed incredulously. 'Husband? You'd have this woman who's been ruined by an unwashed savage? A woman who's been loaned to every other buck that admired her? That's the way they do things, you know.'

Laura shook her head. 'He never let anyone else even touch me,' she protested. 'He loved me, David. I'm not sure you could understand that. As much as I hated being there, being his prisoner, being forced to be his wife, he loved me. He came after me, even though I'm sure he knew it was virtual suicide to ride into Shoshone country after me. I think he chose to die trying to get me back, rather than live without me.'

David snorted derisively. 'Loved you! Those

savages aren't capable of love.'

'Yes they are,' she argued. 'They're not that different from you and me.'

'Not that different from you,' he retorted.

She sighed. 'Well, I guess they are different from you. They would never kill one of their own, or try to. They have dignity and pride and honor.'

His face suffused with anger. 'And you think I don't? Do you think I wanted to kill my own sister? Do you think it was for my own sake I wanted to put you out of your misery?'

'Yes.'

'What?'

'Yes, I think it was purely for your own sake. You couldn't stand the shame of anyone knowing your sister had been a captive of Indians. Had been an Indian's wife. I think it was completely for your own sake you wanted me dead. Then you could just grieve as a noble, heartbroken brother, and have a reason to hate every Indian in the world.'

When he failed to answer, she asked, 'Is that why you planned this whole thing? Were you trying to stir up another war between the Indians and the settlers?'

He seemed to grow a couple of inches as he fired back, 'I'd have succeeded too, if those filthy whores hadn't sold us out. Everybody in the country was blaming Indians. There was a swelling tide of insistence all over the territory for the government to mount a campaign to wipe out the savages

157

once and for all. It was the perfect plan!'

'It was heinous,' she countered. 'Almost as heinous as what you did to all those innocent people. Especially the children. How could you possibly do that to those children, David? Whatever insane hatred could make you do that to helpless, innocent children? Did you rape those women, too?'

'It's the price of war,' he insisted.

'It's the price of insanity,' she disagreed.

'You're the one who's insane,' he argued, almost sounding like a child on a school playground, if you think you can ever live a normal life after being destroyed by all that time with those filthy savages.'

Her response was firm and calm. 'I can, and I will,' she stated.

'That's a fact,' Ansel agreed. 'Matter o' fact, we already got a spot picked out to homestead. My term's up with the army in a couple more months. Laura and I are going to be married. Then we'll build us a place on our own land, and raise a family, and have a home.'

David started to answer several times. His mouth opened repeatedly, but as if struck by some strange form of apoplexy, he made no sound.

The three glared at each other in deep and pregnant silence for nearly a minute, before Ansel said, 'You'd best drop them guns now. You're under arrest for depredations, murder, robbery, and God knows what else.'

David found his voice at last. Ignoring Ansel, he gritted at Laura, 'You cannot be allowed to sully the Cunningham name like that.'

His finger on the trigger of the rifle, aimed squarely at Laura's chest tightened. Before it could fire, however, three shots rang out as one.

The bullet from Laura's rifle caught him squarely in the chest. Simultaneously, the shot from Ansel's pistol entered two inches below his chin, severing his windpipe and shattering his spine. A third shot, fired by the unseen mountain man in the shadows of a clump of plum bushes, entered his left temple and exited the right side of his head.

The combined effect of the three bullets ended any effort of his trigger finger to contract. The rifle fell to the ground, striking the dust a bare instant ahead of the dead body of David Cunningham.

The three survivors stood together, looking at the fallen ringleader for a long moment.

It was Laura who broke the silence. 'I would like to have him buried, Montana. For the sake of my family.'

Montana nodded. 'I 'spect Sergeant Mattern'll bury 'em all. It's more'n they deserve, but I 'spect it's the right thing to do.'

Ansel, ever the practical thinker, was already moving on. 'If you'll take care of Laura for a little while, I'll grab my horse and round up the other horses. Then we can get those women headed back to the hog ranch.'

'Let them walk!' Laura said instantly. Then, just as quickly, she said, 'I'm sorry. You're right, Montana. I can't let myself become like that. That's the kind of thinking that drove David crazy. He was crazy, wasn't he? I mean, not just bad?'

Montana studied her face for a long moment. 'Crazier'n a pet coon,' he agreed. 'I 'spect he done went crazy cuz he loved ya too much ta stand thinkin' of ya as a captive. He warn't respons'ble fer what he done, I don't reckon. Jist went plumb crazy.'

Somehow the idea seemed comforting to Laura. She didn't hear Montana snort at his own words as he turned away. At least it was over, and he could get back to Rain Crow.

He was suddenly overtaken by an overwhelming desire to get back to his wife. 'Last time I'm leavin' her ta go traipsin' around on other folk's business,' he promised himself. 'I wonder if Ansel'n Laura'd like neighbors on thet thar homestead. 'Bout time Rain Crow got thet white folks' house she's always wanted.'